W0259773

Cover Me

SHORT STORIES BY LON OTTO

COFFEE HOUSE PRESS :: MINNEAPOLIS :: 1988

The author thanks the editors of the following publications in which some of these works first appeared: *Luna Tack*, *Minnesota Monthly*, *Mpls./St. Paul*, *Odd Fodder*, *Pomona Today*, and *Vinyl*. "The Bert and Ernie Show" appeared in *Stiller's Pond*, an anthology of upper midwest fiction.

This project is supported in part by Elmer and Eleanor Andersen; Jerome Foundation; Metropolitan Council, from funds appropriated by the Minnesota State Legislature; National Endowment for the Arts, a federal agency; Star Tribune/Cowles Media Company; and United Arts. The publisher also thanks Minnesota Center for Book Arts, where Coffee House has been a Visiting Press since 1985.

Coffee House Press books are distributed to the trade by Consortium Book Sales and Distribution, 213 East Fourth Street, St. Paul, Minnesota 55101. Our books are also available through all major library distributors and jobbers and through most small press distributors, including Bookpeople, Bookslinger, Inland, Pacific Pipeline, and Small Press Distribution. For personal orders, catalogs or other information, write to: Coffee House Press, Post Office Box 10870, Minneapolis, Minnesota 55458.

Library of Congress Cataloging-in-Publication Data

Otto, Lon, 1948-
Cover me : short stories / by Lon Otto.
p. cm.
ISBN 0-918273-40-4 (pbk. : alk. paper) : $9.95
I. Title.
PS3565.T79C68 1988
88-11817
813'.54--dc19 CIP

Contents

For Kathleen

The Circus

"To the circus?" I asked. he nodded sadly, the little boy squatting on his heels, watching me dig the foundations of that summer's home improvement. The building code here requires footings forty-two inches "below grade," the height, exactly, of my belt buckle. When I straightened painfully from hacking at the cool dense clay, ground level barely reached the middle of my thighs, and some of that was piled-up dirt, not "grade" at all. Sweat burned in my eyes, and my forearm and wrist ached, nearly numb from the shock of shovel on stone.

Behind me, attached "where it can be seen from the street," as required, flapped the curling, faded building permit. Pasha, our cat, stared up at it with grim patience – a cat that isn't up to code, having lost three toes in a railroad accident when it was a kitten living on a farm in Michigan.

The boy was one of a pack of kids who hauled supplies in wagons back and forth that summer from their houses to a vacant lot across the alley from our backyard. In the lot, they disappeared up trees, hammering and lashing their possessions to the branches of an overloaded aspen. Digging my ditch, measuring slow progress against the length of my legs, slowly working into the ground, I could hear their howls and arguments: "I own this branch." "It's mine, but you can rent it." Later: "I own this level of branches." "I own everything above this level of branches."

From day to day as they passed by in the alley, they'd ask me what I was doing. "Digging," I'd say.

"Far out!"

One of these was the little kid who squatted now beside the ditch, watching the cat dig delicately in the pile of loose dirt. "What's that cat's name?" he asked. He had never asked me my name.

"It's Pasha."

"Pasha!" He lunged for the cat, which crouched and leaped away in a single whiplike spring. "We had a dog named Pasha!"

"Had?" The boy followed carefully after the cat, which circled back to the diggings and flopped down in the dirt, consenting to be stroked by the humble and appreciative boy.

"We sent her to the circus," he said.

"To the circus?"

He nodded.

"Why the circus?"

"She was getting real old," he said. "I guess my mom got tired of taking care of her. So we sent her to the circus."

The weather-softened building permit flapped in the wind, and the cat sprang up, snapping out of languor into self-important concentration. The boy straightened, ready to leave. "I wish we hadn't've," he said. "I loved Pasha."

But love, though fine, is not enough, I didn't say to him. So in the circus Pasha dances now between the hooves of the great gray and white and dappled circus horses, her grizzled muzzle grinning with the effort under a cockeyed pointed hat.

Dancing upright like no common dog, she springs about, scarcely noticed in the dust and pounding hooves and swirling shapes, scarcely noticing the screaming crowd in the rapture of fulfillment in the circus.

That's where I want to go when I get old, I thought, climbing out of the cold ground into the withering heat of August. *You won't recognize me there*, I told the cat. *I'll be transformed – by the only transformation that I want.*

Slide Show

His father and mother have come to visit them for the first time in their new home. At night, the shade drawn over the picture window displays to passing traffic old photographs of family history. In the darkened living room, the slide projector clicks and leaks light rhythmically while his father and mother step on each other's lines, explaining what was going on.

His parents are veteran, expert antagonists, working over old grudges like virtuosi. The mother is complex, indignant, socially responsible. The father has the car salesman's gift for conversation that floats effortlessly on the surface, stringing puns and jokes and little stories into a cheerful melody he whistles day and night. Retired from his dealership, he has become a collector of old fishing tackle, junked farm implements, used building materials. She longs for dignity and order in her life, closeness in her family's contentious heart.

Pictures of their family homes flash on the drawn shade. A rocky, impossible farm in the middle of Iowa's richest bottom land. A little stucco house in Davenport that his father had built from the ground up. "In my spare time," his father laughs.

His mother stamps in immediately: "You stole that time from your family."

"Look there," he says. "I hadn't even gotten the stickers off the windows yet."

"You stole that time from us."

Finally, a big frame house on a rolling suburban lot. Shrubs gradually surround the house from slide to slide, surging up toward the first-floor windows, eventually overreaching the picket fence. The boy and his brother pose beside the flowering dogwood, in their Sunday clothes. On the front porch, in sun suits. In an inflated wading pool, wearing nothing at all, grinning miserably.

Once there is a SALE sign on the front lawn. In the foreground, a stack of old tires, some cardboard boxes, a card table piled with automotive tools. Leaning against the table, an old jack. His mother recognizes the scene: "That's a fine time to take a picture of our home, with your trash piled up in front of it."

His father says nothing for two more slides, then remarks as if to himself, "I wish I hadn't sold those things. I wish I had that old bumper jack."

"You've got a stinking garage full of them."

"I wish I had that one," he says.

Some of the slides are backward, which he and his mother and father mention but which makes no difference to the daughter-in-law. From outside on the front lawn, these mirrored pictures right themselves – the big hedge on the left, the garage on the right, where they belong. The mother always turns these slides around, just as she inverts those that have been put in upside-down. To her, the change is equally disturbing.

The daughter-in-law shifts uneasily on the sofa. The pictures of her husband as a boy – astride a big dog, at a birthday party, with his brother on a picnic, in a Little League uniform – show him grimacing like a gargoyle, because of his light-sensitive eyes inherited from his mother. You can tell his mother's family, their faces pinched painfully against the unfriendly light.

The pictures of his family's history are surprisingly true in color, even those that are old. Otherwise, the slides are ordinary enough – some blurred, some clear, some showing glimpses of a silvery wooden farmhouse that interests the daughter-in-law a little, until she learns it has long since been torn down.

But in one shot something draws her up past the tense discord of his parents' commentary. "Show that one again."

"This one? That was on our vacation West."

"Best car I ever owned," his father says. "I wish I had that old Buick today."

"You couldn't pay for the gas today. We couldn't afford it then. Your family made sacrifices for that car."

"I wish I had it today – 1938 Buick. Be worth a fortune."

The daughter-in-law leans forward from the sofa, and after the slides have been put away and they all have gone to bed, she lies in the darkness, not listening to the muffled sounds from the next room, the murmur of his parents' steady, practiced anger, which occupies the full attention of her husband, lying stiffly beside her. She sees instead the mountain road, the enormous yellow automobile stretching across the bottom of the frame, a narrow rainbow towering overhead. In the rainbow's cup, the sky is gauzy, gray; outside, deep-water blue, boiling and rolling with blunt-edged clouds.

There are no human figures, yet it is not that that draws her to this picture over all the other portraits of his family history. Rather, it's that the moment seems something fine and whole and peaceful, lodged like a sapphire in a family history ragged with resentments too perfectly remembered in the unnatural vividness of the color slides.

And when, the following day, sheer tension and frustration send his mother to the hospital, the image of the rainbow rising over the imperial yellow car sustains the daughter-in-law in the waiting room, sustains her in the hope that something good will come from the history of the grotesque sun-blind child lying unasleep beside her in the darkness.

We Cannot Save Him

HE WAS OUR FRIEND, WE MISS him. But how were we to know when we laid our hearts in his hands, gave him our faith and admiration, that he would become what he is today, what we see already as we wait for him, half-asleep in these dew-drowned bushes?

We miss him, who still unseen approaches, running with calculated prissy breaths above the foggy river. Before he rounds the brushy curve, we see him, his French running shoes, his shorts, his naked legs, his T-shirt advertising something unimaginable, his terry sweatband, his stopwatch, his tiny nylon wallet fastened to his shoe ingeniously with Velcro – who once was never seen without a coat and necktie – hairy wool, rumpled linen, bleached-to-the-bone starched cotton broadcloth, stained shimmering reptilian silk – who hated zippers as much as polyester, snaps as much as leisure suits.

He was our friend, who traveled by a subway so dangerous and obscure that no one anyone knew had even heard of it, with whom alone we roared beneath the Mississippi, the ancient train crawling with the scum that cities full of hope and happiness generate according to some inverse law of social physics. With him we were horrified and unafraid. He was our friend, he led us clanking underground from the mildewed cavern of the old St. Paul Lower Market to the now-abandoned depths of the Fur Exchange in Minneapolis, and we miss him, who has a sticker on his car bumper, I'D RATHER BE RUNNING, who has a bumper now, who hated cars.

We miss a whole elegant landscape of decay, the rich overlay of stagnation. It was he, himself, who pointed out the first faint trail parting the grass of the hitherto untroubled parkway along dotty, lilac-lovely Summit Avenue. We see him still, as he crouched suddenly under the lamplight, directing our attention to the barely visible spine of earth showing through the grass. We touched the packed soil uneasily where he pointed out the ominous ribbed print of an early, clumsy running shoe. (This was before any of us had ever seen a "jogger," but we had heard of them and knew what their spoor must mean.) We wanted to smash the bottles we were carrying home, to sow the path with glittering denial, but he smiled his disquieting smile and led us away, knowing we were lost. Later, when the path had doubled, then doubled again under the tread of runners, had grown into a freeway of sappy health, then we discovered our defeat's full depth.

We miss him, who understood the secret night squalor of these too facile, too habitable two cities, who recognized by voice and vice the fierce-smelling grizzled crocks whose slapping overshoes crunch down the frozen alleys behind loft-converted warehouses where city planners toast their luck with California wine, where young architects and M.B.A.s and developers plot their clean and devastating lives over alfalfa sprouts and tofu.

He was our friend, we know he knows no fear and will not listen to the warnings we hopelessly recite: the jarred spine, ruined cartilage, wrecked knees and ankles, fractured shins, the mysterious sudden heart attack in the bloom of life, the neck broken on the expensive beach, the thugs waiting with chains and clubs in the inhuman, unmoving early hours of morning. And we whisper to ourselves, *He must not run along the river road at dawn, we cannot save him.*

We miss him, he was our friend, who spoke intelligently in the smoking darkness of the last free-lunch bar in South St. Paul, ripe with the reek of stockyards, spoke of Breton curb dancing, late Aztec erotic dentistry, the Parsee epitomes of the sixth century, who now subscribes to *Runner's World*, who jabbers eagerly about vitamins B and E, the relative merits of Tiger's Milk and Pro-Vita, about how good he feels about himself since he stopped smoking and drinking and eating red meat, who was our dark friend.

We have frozen in our heart's eye an image that humiliates and hardens our resolve: on the silent off-color television bolted above bottles, a mob of marathoners flows over the Lake Street-Marshall Avenue bridge, a river of specks streaming from nowhere to nowhere. Then, in close-up, we see him, captured randomly, neither first nor last, then gone, a number on his chest, who could explain with precision what went wrong with Horsley Beer after the retirement of brewmaster Koenigsberger and the ascendancy of Schlee, and who is now addicted to the mindless, unsubtle high of oxygen starvation and pheromones.

He was our friend, we would warn him if we could. Any moment now he will appear, cheerful in his shorts and flashy shoes against the gray dead end of night, obliviously trotting toward us where we wait, miserable, hidden precariously, the Mississippi's bank sloping treacherously away beneath our feet, our sticks and greasy chains and lengths of pipe oppressive in our hands, warning silently, hopelessly, *He must not run along the river road at dawn, he must not run along the river road at dawn, we cannot save him.*

The New Way

ON THE COLDEST NIGHT OF the year, she taught him a new way to kiss. "Like this," she said, as they lay on their sides, facing each other under the extra blankets. He kissed her like that. "You see what I mean?" she kept saying between the new kisses.

"You bet," he answered, "mmmm," thinking it wasn't entirely right that she should be teaching him a new way to kiss after they had lived together for almost two years.

It was good, though – "You see what I mean?" – largely, he thought, because she was so pleased with herself, getting quite worked up. And though it was very late and she had to be up early the next morning and hadn't been feeling at all well, only the prospect of a trip to the medicine cabinet or his dresser in their icy room discouraged them from anything more involved than hugging and kissing the new way under the heavy blankets.

When they had grown quiet, nestled together, breathing the cold that had gotten ahead of their new wood stove for the first time that winter, they became aware of an engine running somewhere nearby, in the alley below the window or in the side street. A tow truck hauling a wreck to the car-repair shop? It was staying there too long. A snowplow? It hadn't snowed in days. A semi? An armored car? A tank? They heard the hollow, tin-chicken squawk of a loudspeaker then, incoherent but insistent. This from the fire station, a block away? They had never been able to hear its loudspeaker in winter.

He sat up, went to the window, raised the shade. Fire. He saw fire in an apartment building across the avenue. She joined him at the window. They stood there unshivering in the first thrill of tragedy and, through clear spaces in the iced-over window, peered at the flames crawling out of a second-story rear window. Apparently they were fighting the fire from the front of the building. She thought she saw someone – a policeman, she said – going up a ladder into the blazing window. A policeman? He thought he saw a stream, a river of water shooting over the building from somewhere behind the tree that partially blocked their view. She thought it was the horizon.

The cold caught up with them then, and they scrambled back under the covers. They lay talking about the people who lived in the burning building, about frozen water mains, about their own inadequate house insurance, the wood stove he had installed that fall and was afraid to have inspected, the expensive dry oak cordwood burning in the darkness below them, the smoke alarms and extinguishers they kept meaning to buy. After a while he sat up again and leaned over to look out at the parked fire truck, a rescue vehicle, which was all he could see from there.

"Are you going over?" she asked, her voice muffled by the blankets pulled up to her eyes.

"What would be the point?" he said. "It's too damn cold." He lay back, then got up and began dressing, clumsily, in the dark. She switched on the light. "Care to join me?" he asked, knowing she would not.

She drew the covers back up over her nose. "You tell me all about it." And as he clumped down the stairs, she called after him, "I hope the people are all right." He said he hoped so too. He felt responsible.

Their cat slipped out the door as he stepped onto the back porch. He had forgotten to put the cat in the basement for the night, and it must have been sleeping by the stove. "You'll be sorry," he said. The cat ran past the bench where it customarily stopped to let itself be caught and carried back inside. Instead, ignoring the cold, it ran in somebody's boot prints to the middle of the yard, stopping only when it knew he couldn't catch it. Normally it hissed at the cold, hated the snow. Now it just shook its paw and looked up at the moon. "You'll be sorry," he said. "You see what I mean?"

He walked past the fire station, which was across the avenue from the burning building. Three firemen, encrusted with ice, were going into the station, presumably to warm up. "Lucky," he thought, "having the fire so close." It was the first time he'd seen them in their fire-fighting coats and boots and helmets. Generally when he saw them, they were in the alley in shirt sleeves, sanding down rust spots on their cars or grilling steaks. He knew he would not ask the firemen anything about the fire. He felt guilty about being there as a spectator and hoped they wouldn't recognize him.

When he reached the burning building, he saw that the flames were no longer shooting out of the window. He felt guilty again, this time for his disappointment.

They were fighting the fire from the front of the building, as he had guessed. It was all the way he had said it was. A towering snorkel, raised from one of the trucks, was pumping a solid beam of water over an intervening apartment building, the trajectory indeed as flat as the horizon. Another truck was shooting in water from farther down the street. He was astonished that so much water and such cold had not already snuffed the fire, which was now burning throughout the front of the second story, visible on and off behind the huge drifting cloud of steam and spray. He wished he had brought his camera, then decided it wouldn't have worked properly in such terrible cold anyway.

He watched from across the side street, not wanting to get in the firemen's way, not wanting to be told to move along. He stood a little hunched over in his long dark coat, feeling like a victim, imagining that the few people shivering in the cold with him – a dozen happy children, a half-dozen adults – were witnessing a disaster that was personal to him alone.

A bus stopped a block away to let someone off before detouring around the barricaded, hose-entangled avenue. A man sprang out of the bus and raced with unnatural surefootedness down the river of new ice toward the burning building. The man gestured hysterically to the firemen standing around beside the trucks. Then he disappeared into the adjacent apartment building.

He would see this man the next morning, banging ice off the trash cans between the two buildings. "Morning, son," the man would say, walking over to him when he saw him standing in the alley, looking soberly at the blackened building, the cold blue sky visible through the shattered windows. "They're abroad in the land," the man would say, a pleasant-looking man with strange long ears. "They're on the loose," the man would say, nodding grimly toward the charred icy hulk.

"It was set?"

"So it seems. They're on the loose."

Now, in the dark, with smoke billowing into the floodlights, one of the snowmobile-suited children who had been talking to the firemen across the street ran back to report to her mother. He edged casually to within earshot. A fireman had been slightly injured. Several residents had been taken to the hospital, but they would be all right.

He moved off, feeling good that no one had died in the blaze, pleased that he had some information to take home. As he approached the burning building, the great stream of water was shifted downward, to shoot more directly into the flaming windows. Clouds of steam and smoke and fine spray drifted across him, stinging his face with the cold. He shivered there awhile, as long as he could stand it, wondering if his clothes would smell smoky.

Finally the orange windows went gray, then dark. Although the driving water continued to pour into the charred, unthinkable interior, the fire was clearly out. His toes numb by now, he walked back, across the avenue, through the alley behind the fire station, the packed snow squeaking underneath his boots with the complicated voices of small animals.

The cat, which had been waiting on the porch, flowed in past his legs when he opened the door. It disappeared into the darkness of the house, heading for the basement, where it belonged. "You see what I mean?" he said.

She was asleep when he got into bed, but she half-woke and rolled over to face him and asked him what he'd seen. He told her. The position of the trucks: here and here and here, pumping water from overhead. The state of the fire: extinguished. The condition of the building: gutted. Of the trees in front: broken by ice. Of a parked car: crushed by one of the trees. Of the residents of the building: saved.

"That's good," she said, rolling over again while he settled against her, trying to warm up. "You smell like smoke," she murmured.

"No, I do?" But she was asleep. He kissed her before sliding into sleep himself, kissed her in the old way, since the new way depended on both parties being awake. He fell asleep then and did not dream, and downstairs in the stove the coals he had forgotten to bank glowed a furious cherry red before dying, long before daylight, going slowly cold.

The Fellin Sisters: A Story of Animal Passion

AMONG THE CONFUSIONS OF my youth, none comes as often to mind as the Fellin sisters, Katherine and Christine. It was the beginning of summer when they moved into the apartment house where I had been living for four years, ever since I received my doctorate and began working as a laboratory assistant, a job I hold to this day.

From the beginning they fascinated me, inspiring a deep unease. Lithe, blond girls, they spent a great deal of time stretched out in the sun in the grass-cracked asphalt courtyard outside my window. Right outside. Mine is what they advertise as a "garden apartment," meaning basement, with small windows at ground level.

On sunny weekends, sometimes all afternoon, I would keep to the dark inside walls of my rooms, wondering if they could see in as they lay on their flat, tan bellies, chins resting on forearms, seeming to peer in at me whenever their great, green, almost orientally slanted eyes were not closed in sleep. From time to time, one would roll over and rub the other with suntan lotion, moving from her own thighs and arms and stomach to her sister's back and calves and ankles, the distinction between their bodies somehow obscenely insignificant. The first Sunday after they moved in, I watched them from my darkly inefficient efficiency closet kitchen, automatically eating my lunch of crackers and cottage cheese all afternoon, making myself sick, watching as if hypnotized.

That summer was to be the most dismaying time of my life. I made a point of paying visits on sunny days to my lady friend, Melissa, for fear that she might come over and observe the spectacle outside my window. Right outside. Only when it rained would I have her visit me, the dark coziness of my little apartment all the more pleasant for the storms outside. Yet even then I was always conscious of the Fellin sisters in the apartment next door.

Increasingly I lived in fear that Melissa would run into them in the hall some day. But I met them first, several weeks after they'd moved in. Their door stood ajar, one of a string of loud, obnoxious boyfriends having just left. At ten in the morning. In spite of myself, I glanced in as I hurried by on my way to pick up the Saturday mail. One of the sisters, the one with a trace of red in her blond hair (I later learned that this one was Christine), was lounging on their shabby, tattered sofa, her eyes half-closed, mechanically combing her hair, a near smile on her lips. She was wearing nothing but what are, I believe, known as shorty pajamas.

As I passed (paused? I truthfully don't know), she looked up, saw me, and with frightening speed stood up and was beside me before I could back away.

"Why, hello," she purred, leaning against the door. She was practically naked. "Come in. My, we're shy, aren't we." She had a low, soft voice that seemed to bear no relation to the tremendous shrieks and shouts that passed between the two sisters and through our shared wall several times a day. "Shy but nice," she said, showing her teeth, taking hold of my arm firmly and drawing me into their messy apartment. She touched the hollow of her throat with one of her long-nailed, perfectly manicured fingers. "Real nice." Wearing almost nothing.

"I live next door," I managed to squeak, my voice as uncontrollable as a teenager's. "I'm Stanley Musil."

She shrieked, with laughter, I believe, her grip tightening on my arm. I looked down in confusion. Her unbelievably long smooth legs, slender below the bloused and lacy top. Her sister stepped out of the bedroom doorway, froze when she saw me, leaped back behind the door with a high, startled yelp, then reappeared wearing a long furry bathrobe, smiling as if nothing had happened.

"This here's Stan Musial!" Christine announced, thoroughly amused, thrusting me forward a little toward her sister, who was leering as if it had been I and not she who had been seen.

"Stan the Man!" Katherine purred, gliding toward me, hips swaying in an exaggerated fashion, her bare toes appearing and disappearing underneath the long robe. "My!"

"Musil," I said. "Stanley Musil. With two syllables. Common confusion."

"Stan the Man! My!" Katherine took my other arm in both of her strong-fingered hands, the sharp nails pressing sharply. "My," she breathed again. As if she hadn't minded my seeing her.

I stood there a moment between the two beautiful, almost identical sisters. The first one, Christine, licked the tip of her very pink tongue quickly across her upper lip, and I twisted suddenly away. She had a slightly sour, milky breath. "Have to go now," I called back to them in the hall, before shutting and locking my door behind me.

They got into one of their frequent, brief, savage fights then. I could hear their shrill, spitting insults through the wall as I leaned against it, heart racing breakneck.

As abruptly as it had started, the racket stilled. In a short while, they were outside my window, taking turns brushing each other's hair in the late morning sunlight. I grabbed a wedge of Brie and a baby Gouda from the refrigerator, a loaf of French bread from the cupboard, and slipped out the back door, forgetting, in my confusion, the imported champagne I'd been saving for the day's celebration, the fifth anniversary of my engagement to Melissa.

For the next month, I managed to avoid the Fellin sisters but was driven to gnawing sleeplessness by the unspeakable noise from their apartment, cries and howls that increasingly filled the night, as the number of their boyfriends grew. The shouts and obscenity of the idiots fighting among themselves in the alley behind the building were bad enough, but the horrifying, blood-thickening screams from inside the sisters' apartment were much worse, defying imagination.

Fearing, finally, for the safety of these quite gorgeous, if alarming, young things and reluctant to notify the police without greater certainty of foul play, I decided that I needed visual confirmation of my suspicion that something dangerously wrong was going on.

I was unwilling to lurk like a pervert outside their windows, exposed to embarrassing notice or actual apprehension, likely to be fatal, by one of the ever-present gang of suitors. Therefore I carefully removed an already loose piece of baseboard molding and, working quietly and quickly when the sisters were out, cut an opening through the two layers of plaster and lathe, then delicately chiseled a neat tiny hole through the baseboard on the opposite side of the wall, taking care that all the chips remained on my side of the hole and that the molding could instantly and invisibly be replaced. I remembered enough from my brief encounter in their apartment to know that the opening on their side would be in an obscure corner.

The work took only a few hours. That night, while I was finishing my supper of Camembert and rye, I heard the pounding on my neighbors' door, a sound that never failed to set my heart pounding in response.

"The door's unlocked," someone shrieked. It always was. The pounding was more a barbaric ritual than a request for admission. Loud drunken laughter. Shouting. The sound of bodies brushing against the random furniture. Then silence, held breath. Then the tremendous, growing wave of moaning and howling.

Having extinguished all the lights, I scurried on all fours to the loose section of baseboard. There, lying on my side, I peered into the tunnel of light from the Fellin sisters' sinister, chaotic apartment. For a long time, I watched the looming movement of limbs and bodies, swinging into, then out of my narrow funnel of vision, the cries and inarticulate whimpers rising and falling with the fragmentary flashes, lunging and covering, sliding away.

When they were done, the mine of light gone finally black, I rolled over onto my back, racked suddenly by the agony of my long-motionless, stiff muscles. I lay there in the dark, eyes closed, sweat drying on my face, watching the lights of passing traffic float across the wall, trying as coolly and reasonably as possible to reconcile what I had seen with Melissa's and my careful intimacy in the many layered privacy of darkness, secrecy, silence, and restraint. No reconciliation was possible. I was living with animals.

When I woke, cold and rigid on the floor, I replaced the baseboard, nailing it down for good. In the hallway, I found that one of the boyfriends had urinated against my door – not for the first time. As usual, I cleaned up the mess as best I could, not bothering to complain to the landlady, a transplanted old farm woman, who for some reason had never liked me and who was convinced, against all the evidence I could have given her, that the Fellin sisters were ideal tenants.

She would bring them little treats. They would go respectful and affectionate for her, sucking up, then criticize and ridicule her when she had gone. When I would try to dart past unnoticed while she stood cooing to them in their open doorway, she would scowl at me with wildly unreasoning prejudice, and the sisters would smile at me their whitest, hungriest, most hypocritical smiles.

The situation was intolerable, yet I was reluctant to move.

I am a creature of habit, and I liked my place. And so I did what I always do when I have a problem that defies ethical, reasonable solution: I mentioned it to my cousin Rhett, a big vulgar lout, a disgrace to the family, whom I normally avoid like the plague, though we work in the same laboratory. In fact, it was I who had gotten him the job, when he was out on parole and nobody wanted to hire him. You could hardly blame them. He had been doing time for grain robberies from the Minneapolis mill where he had been employed as a night watchman. He had gotten his sentence reduced by squealing on his accomplices, but that didn't help him on the job lines. Before I got him into the lab, the only work he had been able to pick up had been strike breaking, but labor relations around here are notoriously good.

Though he owed me a favor, it was Rhett's fondness for dirty work that led me to hope for help from him. Gratitude was not included in his narrow range of emotions. And so at lunch I mentioned my little problem with the Fellin sisters. I even offered him half of a piece of Stilton that was far too good for him. I had no appetite, anyway. His solution, as usual, was deplorable and dangerous. I am sometimes amazed and always depressed to think that we are related. Yet he is closer to me than the Fellin sisters ever could be. Rhett took me after work to visit an acquaintance of his, Bobo Kane, whom he had met in the penitentiary, one of the few fellow convicts on whom he had not snitched and so counted as a friend. Bobo was a simple-minded brute, a ruined former heavyweight boxer with a huge squashed-in, slobbering face. On various occasions he had done time for second-degree murder, rape, and assault with intent. A creature born in somebody's nightmare.

At Rhett's suggestion, I picked up a couple of steaks for Bobo in order to ensure our welcome. "Me he likes," Rhett said. "But you?" I followed his advice.

We found Bobo slouched on a broken-down sofa on his front porch. Queasily I handed him the bloody package, and we engaged in what might have passed for conversation sometime early in the Pleistocene. Grunts and growls from Bobo, nervous squeaks from us.

After a while Rhett jerks his bright beady eyes at me knowingly. "Those neighbors of yours," he prompts, leering and impatient. "Really something, right?"

"Right," I mumble. Swallow. Rise to the business. "Real lookers," I say. "You should see them sunbathing, wearing almost nothing. Almost naked. Blondes."

He likes blondes, Bobo says. I gathered as much from his reaction, spittle running down his massive, inhuman chin, stubble black against his thick white skin. He likes blondes, he repeats.

I feel unwell, dry-throated, a migraine coming on, but I go through with it – it's what I've come for, bearing raw meat as a gift. "Lots of action," I say, giving their apartment number, repeating it. I recall thinking it fortunate that they had a basement apartment, with a number of only one digit.

He *likes* blondes, Bobo says again, the huge muscular mass of his body stirring with intention, with a gathering of the will, though with nothing that could be described as an idea. He scratches behind a drooping mangled ear. "Pussy," he rumbles, a new expression slowly emerging from around his eyes. "Nice pussy," he growls, starting to grin.

Loathing obscenity, I wince but go through with it. I feel terrible. Stand up. Motion to Rhett that we have to leave. Say it. "Those crazy sisters," I say. Say it. "Those crazy blondes," I say, "they leave their door unlocked at night! Never bother with keys." I leave then, unable to look at Bobo's terrible mouth. Rhett races after me, delighted, and is not offended when I tell him to get lost.

That was a long time ago. Three or four tenants of the apartment next door have come and gone, none particularly memorable. After all these years, I still sometimes lie awake, thinking of the Fellin sisters, the wreckage I returned to after spending an awful night at Melissa's place, returned to the scene my imagination had been drowning in all night. The police, the reporters, the landlady too shocked to be shocked at my slipping in, unkempt, at that hour in the morning.

Sometimes, lying here beside Melissa, her little round ears

as soft and lovely as ever, her delicate nose quivering slightly in sleep, sometimes still I remember the Fellin sisters, Christine and Katherine, remember them with something like regret.

His Palm

From her upstairs window, she watches him move about the yard, tugging the hose after him as he waters their new flower beds and vegetables and struggling hedge, all of it going indistinct in the darkness falling late on midsummer's eve. The friends who had come over for dinner have left early, nervous about their fretful constipated baby. And so the evening that had begun busily, full of conversation and the preparation of food, now spreads out in front of her with an unexpected openness. Dishes washed, food put away, dining-room chairs brought in from the porch, nothing more needs to be done. The house below her, around her, is spotless. They cleaned all afternoon.

She waits for him to finish and come in. He seems about to stop, then remembers the little apple trees, then the new patch of sod, then the flowers in back of the garage. He seems to her to belong to the yard, the yard to him. She feels separated from it and from him, though it was she who had planned and planted the flower beds and the garden and taught him the difference between zinnia and marigold, petunia and pansy, calla and canna.

They would talk that night about having a baby of their own, would play through the familiar litany of risks and richness, love and luck. And she would think of the child, playing in the yard, irritable, past bedtime, and the father, moving a sprinkler, edging a sidewalk, reluctant to come in, until finally the baby starts to cry, swarmed by mosquitoes.

Noticing her framed in the tall rectangle of bedroom light, he waves up at her, his palm in the darkness a pale signal of faithfulness or surrender.

Winners

AT FIRST WE THOUGHT IT WAS a floating plastic bleach bottle, maybe somebody's illegal minnow-trap marker tangled in the lilies. It might have been a clump of the lily pads themselves, flipped over by the wind, their pale undersides glaring in the late-morning sun. We didn't recognize what it was until we were almost on top of it, our boat nosed into the weeds that were keeping it from washing ashore. Keith and I looked at each other.

This was the summer after my parents got divorced. My father had taken me and my best friend on a fishing trip to Rhinelander, Wisconsin, where there was a contest in progress at Schramm's Sporting Goods. While Dad was paying for our licenses, Keith and I had checked out the refrigerated glass case in front of the store, with the leading bass, northern, muskie, walleye, crappie, lake trout, and sunfish lying frozen on a bed of chipped ice. The prizes for each category were displayed in the front window, from a stiff muskie rod and heavy reel with star drag and oversize handle down to a delicate fly rod and tiny reel, which some sportsmen evidently used to catch sunnies.

"What was the prize for walleye?" Keith asked now, peering over the side of the boat.

"I don't know. That Penn Silver Eagle and a Stratoflex, I think. Christ, this would have won easy."

It was the biggest walleye we'd ever seen, eight or nine pounds, we guessed, floating belly up, white, and a little bloated, so it rode high in the water. The turtles hadn't gotten to it yet, as far as we could tell, but who knew what we'd find on the dorsal side. The turtles usually start on the tail, though, and that seemed still intact.

"If we'd caught this baby, we'd be set. We'd've been winners for sure."

Keith said, "Let's do. Let's catch it." And he reached for the landing net.

"We can't," I said. "We'd never get away with it. It's already dead."

"You see any live fish in Schramm's display case? That crummy little walleye in there – was it alive?"

"You got to *catch* them, man. They write up what lure you used and everything."

"Okay." He lifted his rod, cast the jitterbug toward open water, and slowly retrieved it, the lure wobbling and bubbling across the surface in that fat, juicy action that is always so satisfying, even when nothing is biting. He paused, teasing it every once in a while, and led it slowly up to the walleye's mouth. He jiggled the lure against the closed bony plates and yanked hard, setting the hooks.

"Got it!" he screamed. The hooks were on the outside, but it sometimes ends up that way even with living fish. "Net him, man, before he gets away! God, what a fighter!" As Keith hauled the big stiff fish this way and that, churning the water, I reached for the net and scooped it underneath the walleye's tail. Dad had taught me always to net a fish headfirst, especially one as big as this, so that when it jumps, it just gets in deeper, but this guy wasn't going anywhere. I lifted it with effort, half the fish sticking out awkwardly, and hoisted it over the gunwale. Keith helped by pulling up on the line. We lowered it between us.

"I thought it might just fall apart, " I said. "But it's still pretty good."

"Damn right," Keith said. "It's almost perfect." The dorsal fin was splayed up like a sail, chewed here and there, but nothing worse than a long and strenuous life might have done. The huge eyes were a beautiful milky color, and the scales were about five shades lighter than they should have been, except where some little black things were growing. The mouth, I saw, wasn't really closed but gaped open a little, exposing the tiger's teeth that are always a surprise in such a studious-looking fish as a walleye.

I was beginning to think it might work, we'd get away with it, we'd be winners. Then Keith gave that sickening laugh that was one of the reasons why most people at school didn't like him too much. "I was just thinking," he said. "What if the mouth opened up some more, sort of real slow, and then an enormous leech or something crawled out?"

I was used to Keith, and his sense of humor didn't bother me, except that I started worrying again. "How long do you think it's going to last?" I asked. "Maybe we should get it back in the water, so it'll stay cool." We pried out the hooks, which hadn't sunk in past the barbs, and jammed the point of my stringer through the soft part just behind the hard lips. Then we heaved it over the side and tied the other end of the stringer to an oarlock. I cranked up the outboard (this was the first summer that Dad let me handle a motor by myself) and took us in slowly, the high-riding walleye plowing across the wake like a battleship.

Nobody was around the dock when we tied up, so we lugged the walleye up to the cabin, laid it in the shade, and went inside to get something to drink. Dad had taken the ski boat up a chain of little lakes to the Tomahawk Flowage, where he was going to cast for muskies. Fortunately Keith was thirteen, almost a year older than me, and knew how to drive a stick. We would be able to get to town and back before my father came in.

The dinky freezer compartment of the cabin's refrigerator held only a metal tray of ice, a heavily frosted box of frozen vegetables, and a couple packages of bass fillets. We emptied everything in the freezer into a garbage bag, drank some Cokes, and tossed in the rest of the soft drinks and beers from the refrigerator. It would be enough, we thought, to keep the fish cool.

When we heard some furious barking, we rushed outside and found the resort owner's German shepherd rolling around on top of our walleye. We drove him off by throwing beer cans at him and were relieved to find only minor damage. The scales were torn up along one side, but the commotion had actually squashed down some of the bloated quality, so things were about even.

We loaded the walleye into the garbage sack, arranged the ice cubes and cans and frozen food around it, and carried it up to where the car was parked. I was going to put it in the trunk, but Keith pointed out that it would be hot as an oven in there from standing in the sun all morning. The fish would explode. So we placed it on the back seat, opened all the windows, and headed for Rhinelander, about twenty miles away.

Keith was not really such a good driver, tending to go off onto the shoulder when he laughed and taking turns a little too generously. We were making good time, however, when he slammed on the brakes to avoid hitting a squirrel. You could never tell about Keith: sometimes he would go out of his way to kill something, but at other times he was very considerate. I banged my head on the windshield, and it wasn't until we heard cans rolling around that we noticed the stuff on the back seat had been flung onto the floor and scattered. The walleye's tail was sticking out of the garbage bag, and the smell started to get to us. Keith stopped laughing and drove as fast as he dared, faster than the old Audi had ever been driven, trying to outdistance the odor or blow it out the windows.

When we got to the outskirts of town, a complication occurred to me. "How are we going to share the prize?" I asked.

"What do you mean, 'share'? *I* caught it."

I knew he was kidding, but still it was going to be awkward. "No, really," I said, "what are we going to do? There's only one rod and reel. We could match for it, I guess, or maybe they would give us two of something not so expensive. We don't need anything that fancy."

"I did catch it," Keith said again.

"I netted it," I said, unable to believe he would betray me that way. "That was most of the work."

"You tried to talk me out of it. You said we couldn't enter a found fish in the contest. I don't want any cheap shit. I want that Penn Silver Eagle and I want that Stratoflex." He stomped on the accelerator for emphasis, and we screamed around some old farmer's truck.

"This is *my* trip!" I shouted over the roar of wind. "*My* dad paid for everything. This is *my* car. *I'm* the broken-home kid, and if anyone deserves that prize, it's me! You're just my goddamn *guest*, man."

We were passing the strip of motels, roadhouses, and fast-food joints, and Keith slowed down a little as a concession to the increased traffic, though we were still overtaking everything in sight. He started to laugh, and I hit him as hard as I could on the muscle of his arm. The car bounced up on a divider strip, then swerved back and came to a stop at the entrance of an A&W.

"Okay," Keith said, "lighten up. I was just kidding."

"I knew that," I said. "So what are we going to do?"

Somebody started honking at us to get out of the way. Keith gave him the finger and drove slowly toward town, half on the road and half on the shoulder, thinking. Finally he said, "Okay, here's what we do. You get the Stratoflex, I get the Silver Eagle." I started to protest, but he slapped his hand over my mouth. "Wait. We keep them together, though. We take turns using them – me on odd days, you on even days. When we get enough money saved up, you buy a new reel and I buy a new rod." He slammed the steering wheel decisively.

I had to admit that it was a good plan. "But I want the Silver Eagle. You take the Stratoflex."

"Done."

"You take even days, and I'll take odd."

He shook his head. "No way, man. I got to have odd."

"Why?"

"I just have to, is all."

I agreed to take even days, and we drove the rest of the way into town and parked right in front of Schramm's. We dumped out the cans and frozen foods that were still in the garbage sack, pushed the fish back in, and carried it into the store. When we passed the display case out front, Keith gave a thumbs-down sign to the five-pound walleye lying there on ice.

It was almost noon, and the store was pretty crowded, but people gave us plenty of room. An old guy came up then – Schramm, I guessed – and asked what was going on. He was one of these really big guys who are always a little bent over, like bears. Keith dropped the sack onto the floor, pulled out the walleye, and laid it on the sack. Schramm backed off a step and swore into his hand.

"We're entering it in the contest," Keith said.

"Are you crazy? Get that damn thing out of here." The fish really didn't look as good as it had an hour or so before, but you could still tell it was a walleye.

"I know it took us a little too long to get this baby in," Keith said, "but it's got four pounds on that walleye out there, easy. Nothing's going to beat this fish."

"I can't put that piece of carrion in my display case. It looks like it's been dead in the water for a week. Where are your parents, boys?"

I said, "My dad's over at the courthouse, filing some sort of brief. He said that since we caught the fish, we should collect our prize."

Schramm stared down at the fish, keeping his hand over his mouth and nose. While we were standing there, three or four people came in, sniffed, and backed out. A couple of men were looking at what was going on, but they were keeping their distance.

"God almighty," Schramm gasped at last. "Look, I'll give you five bucks for the effort. But get that thing out of here."

"Like hell!" I said. "That Silver Eagle alone is worth fifty. We want the whole deal. We're winners, man. So pay up."

Schramm looked up and saw a little group of customers and clerks gathering at the far end of the aisle, where they kept water-skis and coils of bright yellow tow rope. "Look, son," he said to me, "maybe you better leave and come back with your father."

"He said we should take care of it ourselves. He's real busy."

"Even if the fish was fresh," Schramm said, "the contest isn't over for another three days. Something bigger could come in."

"So we'll wait," Keith said. "Put this monster in the case, and then we'll see if anything can beat it. Nothing's going to beat it--you know that."

One of the customers gagged suddenly and ran for the back door. A couple of the men laughed, in a low, choked fashion. Schramm cursed painstakingly under his breath. He went behind the cash register, rang it open, and took out some bills. He came back and said, "I'll give you each ten dollars. That's twenty dollars for a stinking sack of garbage. Take it and get the hell out of here, or I'll throw you out."

Keith and I looked at each other and shrugged. Schramm shouted, "Eddie!" One of the clerks who had been watching from the water-ski aisle came forward, holding a handkerchief over his nose.

"Need some help, Mr. Crane?" he mumbled into the rag.

"Take this out back and bury it."

"Where?"

"Deep! Now!"

While Eddie, breathless, gathered up the huge fish in the garbage bag as best he could and headed for the back of the store, scattering the onlookers, the big man handed us each a ten-dollar bill. "Don't try this again," he warned us. "Now get out of here. Spend that somewhere else."

When we got out to the car, Keith started laughing. "We did it, man! Twenty bucks!"

"Shit," I said. "That bastard cheated us."

"Come on."

"It wasn't even Schramm," I said. "It was 'Mr. Crane.' We *won* that contest. It's like he stole that rod and reel from us. We were winners, and that son of a bitch cheated us. And we let him do it."

Keith looked down at the ten-dollar bill in his hand as if it were dirt. We climbed into the car in silence, and while Keith drove, I twisted around and retrieved a couple cans of Coke from the mess in back. Keith steered one-handed and took a long pull of the pop. Suddenly he laughed his worst laugh, spurting Coke out of his nostrils, and yanked the car onto a side street.

"I got the perfect plan," he said when he was able to talk again. "We go back right away and see where that guy buries our walleye. Then after dark we go dig it up, break open the display case, and put it in where it belongs. That fat jerk will piss in his pants."

"Forget it," I said bitterly, "just drive," knowing that we were helpless against adult treachery and betrayal. I hurled the half-empty can out the window and watched it tumble, streaming pop like smoke from a crashing jet. "Come on, Keith," I said, "floor this sucker!" The town fled from us in confusion.

Water Bodies

The Gulf of Mexico

He belonged to a Minneapolis law firm that gave sabbaticals, encouraged long vacations, had a policy against staying past five o'clock, and forbade Saturday work entirely. They were refugees from high-powered firms that bred heart attacks like rabbits, divorces like fleas, and they had resolved to keep a healthy balance between their professional and private lives. They rode bicycles, took the bus, packed lunches, talked to their kids. They also made very little money, having difficulty sometimes even meeting their overhead. They were happier than in their former lives, however. Besides, most of them had spouses who brought in second incomes.

All of them broke the rules occasionally. Burney Nichols

was the worst, though. Without children, with a wife who worked long hours herself, Burney found it easier to put in extra hours on the sly than worry about missing deadlines and going into malpractice. He took no more than a week's vacation at a lake cottage each summer, another week or two around the winter holidays, and a few long weekends with Laurel at bed-and-breakfasts in nearby Red Wing or Wabasha or Hastings.

But the spring that Laurel told him she was pregnant, he put in for a month-long vacation in June and bought a bus ticket to Pensacola, Florida. "All right," his partners said, "it's about time. Old Burney is loosening up. But, hey, will you be able to finish Warnke before you take off?"

He didn't tell them about Laurel or about his friends in Pensacola. He left the vacation mysterious, making it seem more spontaneous than it was. In fact, he had long before planned an extended weekend for the middle of the month, when he and Laurel were driving north of Green Bay for her brother's wedding, and their annual fishing trip with Burney's parents fell in the last week of June. He didn't tell them about his father's failing health, the long-checked prostate cancer beginning to assert itself again, and he passed Warnke along to the partner who tended to ask the fewest questions. "Time for a break," he said, leaving the weekly office meeting early to finish packing. "Don't work too hard, suckers."

On Memorial Day, still fuzzy from two days of riding a Greyhound bus, he drove with his friends down to the beach. When he'd arrived the night before, they had given him a feast of fresh shrimp washed down with a sickening local wine made from scuppernongs, and they had insisted that he learn the names of the seven turtles that roamed freely in the bungalow before letting him go to sleep on the floor of their studio. Two of the turtles were familiar. He remembered them from the huge farmhouse in Tennessee that he'd shared for a while with Sal and Vera before returning to Minnesota and starting law school again. All night he heard thick claws methodically clack and scratch on the cool concrete floor, as one or more of the turtles plodded restlessly among Sal's bronze sculptures and Vera's cast-iron printing presses. He hadn't told them he was coming, hadn't told them why he came, scarcely knew himself. He had been relieved and grateful when Sal's gruff, suspicious voice answered the call he'd placed from the Pensacola bus station. He was glad they were home, glad they lived now near a major body of water, where he could swim and think about nothing.

"What's the matter?" Burney asked, as they slogged through the soft drifted sand down toward the shoreline. On the broad white beach that stretched endlessly in either direction, parties of bathers were so widely scattered that the blare of their radios barely crossed each other. "Where is everybody? Doesn't the South have Memorial Day?"

Sal surveyed the scene with satisfaction. "For here, this is a crowd," he said. "Shitty climate so far has saved this part of Florida." Burney looked at him. There was a light breeze, a cloudless sky. It was eighty-five degrees. "It's okay now," Sal admitted. "But the winters are wet, and the summers get hot as hell. Let's go!"

Sal found them a place a little closer than necessary to two women lying face down on a blanket, their bikini tops removed. When one of them rolled over, Vera said, "Well, sure, why not? Nothing there to get anybody excited." Sal tried to talk her into taking off her own top, but she headed toward the water, with Sal and Burney following. When he removed his sunglasses, Burney was sharply conscious of his winter's pallor. He saw nobody on the beach who was not already at least a little tan. The woman's breasts were darker than his arms. He looked like a corpse, and he squinted in pain at the sun's living glare.

The perfect sand sloped gradually into water that was warm and buoyant, with more waves than Burney had expected from the gulf. The three of them horsed around for a while, returned to their blanket for lunch, and lay baking. Vera had brought sunscreen, which she insisted Burney use. He rested his chin on his forearms as Vera spread the cream on his back and shoulders. "This isn't waterproof," she said. "Put more on if you swim again."

Five years before, they had picked him up hitchhiking nowhere in particular, fleeing law school. They had brought him home, given him a room, and put him to work on their hopeless farm. They had healed his anger and confusion, made fear something he could live with, like a bad eye or sinus headaches. It was good to be in their hands again, safe for a moment from the terrors of life and death.

After Sal and Vera dozed off, Burney walked into the water again, walked till the waves reached his crotch, then flung himself forward. He was a strong, clumsy swimmer, hauling himself through the water in a style mastered as a kid in the beachless fishing lakes of Minnesota and Wisconsin. There he had had to swim beyond the drop-offs to reach freedom from the clinging weeds. He would swim across the weed line to deep water and then tread water and float and swim to near exhaustion, before heading back in to some dock or rocky shore. He had hated the passage through that tangle and tickle, that invisible, undifferentiated soft grasping at his ankles and arms.

There were no weeds here. The sand bottom was pure and sweet, but he swam toward the distant line of white, where the big waves from the open sea were lifted until they finally exploded into foam and spray and broke up into the merely man-sized waves that could make it the rest of the way to shore. It looked a little too far, but he wondered what it was like out there. He swam and rested, turned over and squinted into the gas-blue sky, and swam again. When he looked back, he could not make out the sex of swimmers at the water's edge, and instead of children there were only little dark animals scurrying along the beach. There was no sound except the gradually increasing thunder of the breakers that rose like bluffs ahead of him, slowly broadening from a single edge into an expanse of transformation where the ocean floor lifted each wave and heaved it over into the froth of the wave before it.

The line of breakers became a field of breaking, and before

he was entirely aware, Burney was in the midst of it, with roaring and sibilance all around him. He panicked for a moment, tasted salt that still surprised him after hours of swimming in it, floundered, saw nothing flash before his eyes, then felt himself lifted, lifted, then dropped again and lifted. He caught on and lay back and learned to wait and watch and swim easily upward on the swell of each wave until the frothing crest rushed past, then drop with the trough and wait again.

Time stopped, there was nothing but pure, sexual, abstract movement. It was easy. He could scarcely see people on the beach, he was so far out and the glare was so fierce. He could not sink. He was not even swimming. It was easy, pure freedom, the first absolute and effortless harmony he had ever known. He would never go back. This was what had happened to the whales, he thought dreamily, lifting his face to the sheer sun, feeling under his body the living sea. He was enchanted. He would never go back.

He went back. By midnight he wished he were dead, writhing in the furnace of the worst sunburn of his life. Vera's prescription-strength cortisone cream helped a little, and soaking in a tub of cool water and baking soda helped a little, but still it felt as if white-hot needles were being driven into his back. His face swelled, and his hands and feet puffed up till the cherry skin was tight and featureless as overblown balloons. It took two days before he could tolerate clothes, days more before he could wear shoes. Sal made a sketch of him, sitting slumped forward on a kitchen chair, bloated, miserable, wearing nothing but his shorts, watching two of the turtles gnash in slow motion at an old cabbage.

Burney left when the swelling had finally disappeared, though the tops of his feet were still too tender for anything except unlaced sneakers. He left in the morning, taking the bus along the coast road to New Orleans, where he planned to wander around for the rest of the day and then catch a late bus north.

He hiked from the New Orleans bus depot to Jackson Square and began systematically crisscrossing the French Quarter, shuffling back and forth between Canal Street and Esplanade, each time turning a block farther north. He went into cafés and bars when he wanted to rest, and he checked out every antique store he passed, looking for a present for Laurel. Everything he saw was too expensive or too bulky to carry on the bus, but late in the afternoon, in the back of a densely jumbled shop, he found a blackened, crudely carved wooden cat, warped and split, worm-eaten, that was one of the most wonderful things he'd ever seen. Its eyes squinted demonically, and its great grinning mouth was studded with long yellow peg teeth. Something apparently had once chewed on its head, for the ears were reduced to irregular frayed stumps. The shopkeeper told Burney that it was Egyptian, which seemed improbable enough, though it did have the upright sitting posture of ancient Egyptian cat statues. It was truly hideous, the owner agreed, and he charged Burney only thirty-five dollars for it and wrapped it in newspaper and a grocery bag.

While eating a poor-boy sandwich in an almost empty saloon, Burney unwrapped the cat and set it on the table in front of him. The young black man tending bar hollered over to him, "What's *that*, man?"

"It's a cat."

"It look like the devil."

Burney reached the walled St. Louis Cemetery around dark and turned back, weaving south this time, skipping streets of lesser interest. He peered into the doorways of strip joints as he passed them, and at the corner of Dumaine and Royal he stopped and went back to find a club on Bourbon Street that had advertised nude dancers and no cover. One other man was at the long bar, ignoring a young woman dancing by herself on a little platform covered with turquoise indoor-outdoor carpeting. Burney ordered a glass of beer, for which he was charged three dollars and fifty cents, and stood at the bar drinking it, casually watching the woman dance and peel off one piece of clothing after another. They were regular clothes – tank top, shorts, panties – nothing exotic, nothing with sequins or spinning tassels. There was a large mirror behind her, and by the time she wore only a G-string, which did have the grace of a little fringe, she kept turning toward the mirror, studying herself, as if she were a girl dancing in her own bedroom.

When the music stopped, she gathered up her clothes and left the platform, disappearing into the darkness at the far end of the bar. Another woman took her place, also dressed as if she had just come in off the sidewalk, and Burney prepared to go, feeling fairly stupid but with his curiosity satisfied. As he turned to leave, the first dancer, dressed again, came up to him and asked if he'd liked her dancing and if he wanted to give her anything to show his appreciation. He said he thought it was fine and tucked the clumsy package under one arm and fumbled in his wallet for a dollar bill, finding only traveler's checks and a five. He gave her the five, which seemed too much but maybe wasn't, and fled.

He ended up in Jackson Square again. After buying a coffee, he walked down to the levee. He sat on a bench overlooking the Mississippi and thought of Laurel, twelve hundred miles north along this same river, pregnant. By moonlight he addressed a postcard with pictures of voodoo stuff to Sal and Vera, another card to the people in his office, and one to Laurel, which he would presumably beat back to Minneapolis.

The bus was supposed to leave at midnight, but after everybody and their excessive belongings were aboard, they all had to pile out and get on a different bus. No one said why. It was another forty-five minutes before the second bus departed, and by then the crowded passengers were getting raucous. The bus left the station parking lot, drove about a block, then circled back. They were allowed to stay on this time while mechanics worked in the glow of trouble lights under the flap of the engine compartment. A radio that had been bleating in the back was joined by another tuned to a different station. The music stayed on when the driver swung up into his seat once more, but he did nothing to stop it. He ignored the racket and the couple dancing and the reek of cigarette and marijuana smoke drifting forward – ignored the whole set of federal regulations posted above the door, though in fact no one was trying to stand forward of the white line.

A big man moved in next to Burney as passengers shifted around. He was an offshore oil-rig cook, he said, heading home for a few weeks' vacation. He lit a cigar, offered one to Burney, and grunted when Burney declined. "It's self-defense," the man said. "I hate that damn pot." After the cigar was glowing, he reached into his valise and pulled out a bottle. Burney accepted the offer this time, though he didn't like whiskey and was conscious of the man's saliva on the bottle's neck.

It was difficult to understand the cook over the party din shaking the bus, so Burney had to lean over to catch what he was saying about his "nigger assistant" who defended his lousy cooking as being authentic coon ass. " 'Coon ass,' my dick," the cook sneered. "My wife hear him call himself coon ass, she'd cut his lungs out. *She's* coon ass, boy. This is your coon ass," he said, hunching forward seriously. "Your coon ass is raised down on the delta. He's part Indian, part Spanish, part French, part white. It ain't no nigger!" He sat back with a snort and fell asleep and did not wake even when the engine died and the bus pulled over onto the shoulder. The driver got out and disappeared into the absolute darkness. The party went quiet for a moment. Then someone shouted, "We're jinxed!" And the party went wild again.

Burney was thinking about the demonic cat in the luggage rack overhead, when a boy of about nineteen slid into the seat across the aisle from him. The boy seemed unsurprised when it turned out they both were heading for Minnesota. "You like New Orleans?" he asked.

"Sure."

"I hate it," the boy said. He'd come down to work on the oil rigs and had been laid off. "I couldn't've stayed much longer," he said. "You can't *do* anything in New Orleans." Burney would have thought it was the other way around, but the boy explained. "At home you can go anywhere. You get in your car and drive anyplace you want. Here it's all swamps and bayous, they got you trapped." Burney looked past the boy to the dark trees crowding against the bus windows. He supposed they were in bayou country now. It hardly seemed a highway. There was no traffic at all. He thought again about the Egyptian cat's voodoo smile and thought of Laurel and the vague amphibious shape of their baby being formed, and he resolved that if the bus trip didn't straighten out, he was going to pitch the cat into some trash barrel, thirty-five dollars or not. He'd wait till they reached the Minnesota border. Then he'd evaluate how things had gone. He thought of his parents, living a little south of Davenport, and hoped they wouldn't ask him about the trip, why he had come so close to them and not stopped.

The cook woke up when the bus started moving again and talked some more about niggers and coon asses and white trash, and then he pulled an enormous revolver out of his valise, the black barrel glinting under the little reading lamps. "This Bud's for you," he said and laughed. "I got the wife one of these babies too," he said. "She's ready and willing to use it if any scum, black *or* white, comes crawling around while I'm away. *Real* willing. She'd love it." Burney laughed.

The cook got off in a town that was nothing but a darkened filling station, a few houses, and one ancient streetlight casting yellow gloom. When the bus pulled away, Burney looked back and saw the man disappearing down an incline from the highway, as if he and his willing, well-armed wife lived in the bayou itself, like muskrats or alligators. The bus gathered speed again, and Burney stared out at the blank claustrophobic wilderness pressing in on the company of revelers. He had done everything wrong. It would be all right.

Lake Michigan

All the way across Wisconsin, Burney had talked about Sal's sculptures and Vera's new series of broadsides, the mysterious hidden courtyards of the French Quarter, the oil-rig cook, and the buoyancy of the Gulf of

Mexico, but when they reached Green Bay, he grew quiet, concentrating on picking up the highway that would take them north to Sturgeon Bay. Laurel studied his red and peeling profile and wondered what had really happened on his trip. He seemed more relaxed than before, but it was hard to tell why. Maybe he had just needed a break. She wished he wouldn't look so ridiculous at the wedding, however, for she was starting to feel a little dumpy herself and would have liked to arrive with some drama, some romance on her side, some glamour and impressiveness. She stared at a little curl of skin peeling up from the bridge of his nose, and after a moment she reached over and pinched it off.

"Hey!" he protested, his eyes watering from the sudden pain. "Don't!"

"Sorry. I thought it was looser."

"Jesus Christ, leave my skin alone."

Although Laurel apologized some more, stroking Burney's hair in a conciliatory manner, her fingers itched after other little flakes of skin at his hairline and the back of his neck. He looked mangy, and her brother was sure to make some wisecrack about it.

"Stop it!"

"Sorry. I didn't realize I was doing it again."

The car was unbearable after hours in the unrelenting sun, and now, creeping through a neighborhood of narrow streets and brick warehouses, probably lost, late already for the cookout that was to be the opening event of the two-day celebration, even the hot wind of the highway was gone. Laurel sat forward, peeling her soaked blouse away from the seat back. "If we don't get out of town quick, Burney, I'm going to go nuts." She wondered how much of this was hormones, wondered if her metabolism was heating up already and how she would ever endure six and a half more months. She let her blouse dry a little, then flopped back, hooking one arm out the window and the other around Burney's neck.

"Laurel!"

"Sorry."

They pulled into the resort grounds about two hours behind schedule. Mark and a dozen of his friends were lounging around on lawn chairs, drinking, the remains of a picnic scattered about them on the close-mown grass. Burney stopped the car in the middle of the curving drive and found out where they were to stay. Sweating, speechless with relief at finally being in the cool presence of Lake Michigan, they hauled their bags into the little cabin. Laurel was pulling on her swimsuit when Burney brought in the last suitcase. "Who is that frizzy redhead?" he asked, watching Laurel struggle with the straps. "The one sharing Mark's chair. That's not who he's marrying, is it?"

"He's marrying Ann. She's the tall dark one. The redhead's Kim. God, this is tight."

"Kim seems familiar."

"She and Mark used to live together," Laurel said. "I'm surprised to see her here. She was always a little crazy, though. There!" When they went outside again, she headed toward the water.

"Aren't you hungry?" Burney asked. "They must have some food left. I'm sure there's still beer."

"Go ahead," she said, the sand luxurious underfoot. "I'm dying to get into that water."

"It's going to be cold."

"Good."

Lake water was always cold at first. She'd learned that a long time ago. And she'd learned not to prolong the agony but to plunge in as fast as possible, get over the first shock, then relax and enjoy it. She raced into the water, took a deep breath, and dove when the chilly water was still scarcely knee-deep. She scraped against the sand bottom, then swam underwater as far as she could, kicking furiously, relishing the bracing cold. She came up gasping, shaking the hair out of her eyes, and thought she heard Mark and some of the others shouting something at her. Standing on her toes, she could just keep her mouth above water. She waved up at them and would have shouted back, but her jaw felt stiff and awkward. It was really cold. She snorted water out of her nose and swam again, trying to get used to it.

Instead, incredibly, it seemed to get worse. She couldn't believe it, it contradicted all previous experience. She felt her thrashing arms and legs stiffen, felt an unfamiliar tingle in her breasts, felt the unbelievable cold pressing into her stomach and chest, until she realized it would not let go. It was attacking her, her warmth bleeding into the icy water faster than she could replace it. Her toes dug for the bottom, water covered her mouth, her feet kicked against nothing. She was going the wrong way. She looked up and saw the evening sky purple through a hard shimmer of water. Her arms barely moved. Her legs felt heavy and dead. Her heart pounded desperately, trying to make up for everything else. Then her knee touched sand. She stood up in the low sun, shivering wildly, and staggered to dry land.

"I thought you'd gone crazy," Mark said to her when she joined the party. "No one swims here this early in the year."

"It was very refreshing."

"Refreshing, hell. Your lips are still blue."

Laurel had met most of Mark's friends at one time or another, but she knew none of them very well. Ann came from California, seemed shy and happy, content with the peripheral attention everybody else paid her. They were all Mark's friends. Ann's father and mother were flying to Chicago and driving up the next day with Laurel's and Mark's parents.

Kim was sitting at Burney's feet, listening to him tell the stories about the Gulf of Mexico and New Orleans, which Laurel had by heart now. She wondered what Kim was doing there, whether she was going with another member of Mark's group now, wondered even whether she had been invited. It would not be unlike her to show up unasked, a kind of shrill goddess of envy and hysteria materializing at the wedding feast, unwelcome, irresistible. Formerly a little plump, she now was gaunt as a model, electric and beautiful, and it seemed to Laurel that after one more beer Burney's hand would slide helplessly into her pale blaze of hair.

Then Mark's best man grabbed Kim by the wrist and lifted her lightly to her feet, and they headed together toward the distant lodge, laughing, intimate. "Ah," Laurel thought, lowering herself into Burney's lap and accepting a bite of his over-cooked bratwurst. "She's something, hmm?"

"You never liked her much, did you?"

"Not too much," Laurel said.

"She seems nice enough."

"Oh, boy," Laurel said, stroking Burney's broiled forehead, the little frayed edges of skin ticklish to her palm. "Oh, you sweet boy."

That night Laurel woke after only an hour's sleep, gasping, confused, suffocating. She could see nothing, hear nothing. It took her a few minutes to realize what was wrong. All her life, she had lived with streetlights glowing through drawn shades and curtains, headlights sweeping ceiling and walls, traffic sounds growling comfortingly during even the loneliest hours of the night. All her life, she had gone to sleep listening to the deep murmur of truck tires, her dreams accompanied by the song of sirens, soothed by the subliminal vibrations of a living city.

She listened now for crickets, frogs, nightjars, owls – any substitute noise that would assure her she was alive. But either the well-insulated cabin walls shut them out or it was some still point in the creepy natural world, a moment when everything held its breath. She was sure that in rough weather she could have heard waves crashing on the beach, but it was calm and it had been calm. Nothing. Even Burney, who sometimes snored and usually slept restlessly, muttering in his sleep, lay so quiet that Laurel had to jab him a few times with her elbow before he sighed and rolled over.

Laurel lay on her back, listening to the inadequate whistle of her breath through clenched teeth. She caressed her belly, wishing for some stirring, some signal from the lively future. Nothing. Stroked her familiar, faithful sex. Nothing.

Finally Laurel rose, dressed by feel in jeans and Burney's navy-blue sweatshirt, and stepped out of the muffling cabin. To her relief there was moonlight, intense and startling, away from the shadowing birch trees that surrounded the cabin, and cold sweet air. Outside the cabin, she could hear the slap of little waves against the sand. She pulled the sweatshirt's hood up over her head and walked down toward the water, intending to hike for a while at the water's edge, where the sand was firmly packed.

As she rounded the weather-beaten boathouse, Laurel stopped. Somebody was coming toward her, a figure dressed blazingly in white, moving slowly through the deep sand. It was Kim, barefoot, wrapped in a terry-cloth robe that nearly brushed the sand. Mark used to have a robe like that, Laurel thought.

When she reached the shoreline, Kim stopped, stared for a long time at what must have been to her a path of glittering moonlight stretching from her white feet straight out to the deep mystery of the lake. She stood there a long time. Laurel was about to either retreat or step out from the shadow of the boathouse and say something, when Kim dropped the robe to the sand and stood naked in the moonlight, pale, ethereal, her shoulder blades distinct as a cupid's wings.

Laurel crouched a little, tense, resolute in the heavy clothing that made her feel armored and ready to act. But before she could move or even shout, Kim strode like a goddess into the lake, her slender white ankles and calves disappearing into the glistening black water.

Kim took two, three steps, then shrieked and danced back out of the water, while Laurel's own warning cry was still rising in her throat. Kim leaped back onto the beach and collapsed beside the crumpled robe. Furiously she dried her feet and legs. She sprang up and brushed sand from her buttocks and thighs, threw the long robe around herself, and raced back up toward the lodge.

Laurel watched from her half crouch, wondering if she hadn't in fact screamed. She must not have. And afterwards she didn't even need to laugh, the dark silence of the cabin was that perfect.

Rat Lake

Burney said, "He looks so small."

Laurel put her arm around his waist. "It's eating him up, Burney."

"He's not just thin, he's *small.* He's hardly there."

She squeezed. "I know. It broke my heart when I saw him."

They were in a bedroom of the cabin they were sharing for the week with Burney's parents. Al and Mary Nichols had arrived the night before. When Burney's car had crunched down the gravel path behind the cabin, Mary had come out to greet them, and Al, who should have been out in a boat doing a little trolling or rummaging around in some storage shed or up at the resort's tavern finding out where they were biting this year, had waited for them inside, draped in a flannel shirt that once had strained across his chest, in trousers that were as bunched at his waist as a badly furled umbrella, his eyes enormous and perplexed.

"Used to be I'd scarcely see him, sunup to sundown," Mary said to Laurel as they ate supper. "Now I can't get him out of the house. Sometimes I'd like to shoot him."

Al winked at Burney. "Isn't that what I always told you? She griped about me being gone, but who could have borne me otherwise?"

"There's such a thing as the middle ground."

Al winked again. Burney wondered if he was conscious of how dramatic the old gesture had become, now that his face had shrunk away from his dark eyes.

"We Nichols spit on the middle ground, don't we, Burney?" Al said.

"You Nichols spit on the floor, if nobody stops you."

"All or nothing – that's the Nichols motto, right, boy?"

"Then God help you and your poor baby," Mary said to Laurel and rose from the table to crash some pots and pans around in the tiny sink. Laurel began clearing the table, listening for the little signals that would tell her the tension had eased though the argument might continue, the slight shifts of rhythm and undertone that marked the transitions from anger to mere habit and automatic, even affectionate, sparring. She listened.

After supper Burney hauled their fishing tackle down to the boat that came with the cabin, while Al stood on the dock instructing him in simple tasks he had accomplished a hundred times before. With Mary watching from the cabin's screened porch, Laurel and Burney helped Al get into the boat and steadied him while he moved cautiously to the front seat. They thrust a flotation cushion under him, but even then he only stood there, bent stiffly forward a few degrees, knowing he could not sustain the half-squatting posture the boat's low metal seats would impose. "I think I'm done for," he kept saying, bending a little, straightening a little, all the while smoking with steady, rhythmical drags, like some piece of pointless, archaic machinery. "Have these seats always been so low?" he said. "I think I'm done for."

Burney looked helplessly up to the cabin, but his mother had evidently gone inside. Then Laurel noticed her hustling around from the back of the cabin, lugging an aluminum lawn chair. Burney took it from her and positioned it securely in the rounded bottom of the boat, and Al sat down. The webbed seat scarcely sagged beneath him. "Say, this is fine," Al said. "Why didn't I think of this? Thank you, Mary."

"You're going to desert us every evening," she said, already heading back to the cabin. "You might as well be comfortable."

"I feel a little foolish," Al said, when they were well out into the lake. Burney sat at the tiller of an old Johnson outboard, steering them toward the shadows on the western shoreline.

"Those fancy bass boats have seats with backs and everything," Burney said. "This is how it's supposed to be."

"You know what those babies cost?" Al asked, cradling his rod on a lap that was like a scarecrow's. "I talked to an old boy in Davenport who sells them – met him at Rotary – and he said they start at six thousand bucks! Start! I told him I used to catch more bass with a cane pole and frog from a leaky wooden rowboat than those pros nowadays, with all that equipment, ever dreamt about. Did you know that six thousand dollars is ten times a man's annual salary in half the countries of the world? For a bass boat!"

"You could afford one now."

"I'd rot in hell before I paid six thousand dollars for a damn bass boat! I'd be tempted by a good buy on a used one, though. I told that old boy to look out for one. I'd trade horses, I told him." His hands tying a River Runt to the monofilament line were almost fleshless, but they seemed steady enough. "He said nobody sold them much, used. But he's looking out for one for me."

The huge red sun settling onto the tree line blazed into Burney's eyes through his dark glasses, and he felt relief when they approached the shadows along the far shore. There was a good run of lily pads there, but when Burney took the oars and worked them in far enough to be out of the sun, they were almost on top of the weeds.

"What the hell are you doing?"

"Trying to get into the shade."

"*We* don't have to be in the shade – the fish do. Come on, boy."

Burney rowed them out a ways, and from his strangely regal position Al cast awkwardly toward the lilies. His lure splashed a few yards short. "Reel's gunked up," he grumbled. Burney edged closer.

The lake was small enough that even without the binoculars, which Mary was using, Laurel could distinguish the two men outlined against the dark shore. "You want to use these?" Mary asked.

Laurel shook her head. "How's Al doing, Mary? How are *you* doing?"

The older woman kept the glasses fixed steadily on the little boat, which seemed motionless in the flash of the setting sun. "That man's given me a lot of grief. As you know." She didn't move from the window, and her arms, bracing the heavy binoculars, seemed tireless. "The doctor told me he has six months, tops. Probably more like three or four."

Laurel turned from the window, her eyes dazzled by the burning water. The dark living room of the cabin flickered as she turned. She found a lamp that looked suitable for reading, switched on its forty watts, and settled down with the novel she'd been trying to finish for months. The pages looked yellow in the dim light. "I don't see how you can stand it," she said.

Mary lowered the glasses for a moment, not to rest her arms but to fix again where the boat was in relation to the shoreline. "If I could figure any way not to stand it, I would. I'd go to Mars. I just can't figure any way." She raised the glasses. "Is that fool standing up? Damn him! Damn him!"

Burney reached far down into the water with the landing net and brought up the bass, flipping and twisting at the hooks. "All right!" he said. "Pretty good! What do you think – three and a half?"

Al lowered himself toward the lawn chair, misjudged the distance, crashed a little sideways, then settled down, coughing, hacking up phlegm, fumbling for a cigarette. Finally he leaned forward and looked at the fish, slapping around in the bottom of the boat. "About three," he said. "Felt like thirteen. I almost lost it." He watched as Burney slipped a stringer hook through the fish's bony lips and lowered it into the water. "Your basic bread-and-butter largemouth. Okay. That's okay with me."

They fished awhile more, but the pauses between Al's casts got longer and longer. "You want to go in?" Burney asked.

Al was sitting stiffly, had not spoken in quite a while, and was not even smoking. "I guess," he said. When Burney pulled in the stringer with the lone bass before yanking the motor, Al said, "Let me see it, Burney." Burney held up the fish for him, and Al looked at it for a long time in the twilight as it dangled patiently, gills moving in and out, tail curling a little from side to side. "It's a girl," Al said. He had always claimed to be able to sex most species of freshwater fish just by looking at them. Burney had never managed to prove that he couldn't. "Let it go."

"Come on, it's a real good fish. We never let this size go."

"We don't want to fool cleaning just one."

"I'll do it."

"Let it go."

Burney looked at his father's huge-eyed, unfamiliar face, pale gray against the dark trees. He unsnapped the stringer hook, lifted the fat bass by its lower jaw, leaned over, and slid it into the lake. It hung there a moment, considering, then was gone.

That evening Burney played double solitaire with his mother, while Laurel read and Al took his reel apart. He worked slowly, spreading the oily parts out on the newspaper Mary had made him use.

"I hope you have easier deliveries than mine," Mary said to Laurel without looking up from her cards. "Andrew was the worst. I was in labor for thirty-two hours. They stitched me up like I was a football. Then they ignored me for two days. Forgot about me, if you want to know the truth. This was during the war. They didn't care about births, they were too busy murdering each other. I almost died of dehydration."

"That sounds awful," Laurel said.

"Al, of course, was conveniently overseas."

"In sunny Italy," Al said. "The most beautiful place I've ever been, even with all the destruction. I wish I'd had a chance to go back after they'd cleaned it up."

"They kept him in the States for two years after Pearl Harbor, kept sending him home on leaves till he managed to get me pregnant again, then immediately shipped him out, left me completely on my own, with a toddler and morning sickness."

"When we got to Rome, you'd think we'd been on their side all along. They loved us."

"Burney hadn't been much better. He was so restless, he broke my bag of waters two weeks early, and they had to give me a C-section. Didn't have contraction one. That doctor was no artist, either."

"I saw a million dollars worth of pictures in one dirty little garage," Al said. "Nazis were getting ready to haul them back to Germany. Those old boys knew their art, I'll give them that."

Laurel thought of her bag of waters, felt her cells swell, her cartilage soften. She thought about pain. When Mary went into the cabin's tiny bathroom with Al to help him with a sponge bath, Laurel went to the refrigerator to make herself a sandwich. "You want one?" she asked Burney, as he stared down at another hopeless hand.

Before he could answer, there was a thunderous crash from the bathroom. Al had slipped and fallen against the metal shower stall. Mary was on the floor beside him, trying to get him up, cursing herself viciously for having turned away a moment. Burney shoved in past Laurel, who was heading for their bedroom. He looked away quickly from his father's groin, incapable of facing what wasn't there. Pressed up against the sink, he tried to keep out of the way while Laurel and Mary draped an army blanket over Al's unbelievably thin body and helped him to his feet. "Don't let go," Al kept saying in a harsh, panicked voice. "Don't let go, don't let go, don't let go."

Hours later Burney was wakened by the sound of his father bumping around in the sparsely furnished cabin. When he stepped through the curtained bedroom doorway, he found Al shuffling around the kitchen table, clutching its edge, working his way toward a chair on the far side. Before he reached it, Mary came out of the bathroom with a bottle of the liniment relied upon by generations of Nicholses. A moment after she uncapped the bottle, the cabin reeked of its prodigiously medicinal odor.

"Did you bruise something in that fall?" Burney asked.

Al shook his head. "Shoulder. Casting. Hurts like hell." Burney sat across the table from them, while Mary rubbed liniment into Al's bony shoulder and back and neck. Hunched like that, Al's chest appeared caved in, an impression confirmed by his jagged intakes of breath.

Burney felt that it somehow was his fault, that he should have taken better care of his father, should not have let him fish so long. Responsibility settled onto him like a heavy bird and made him awkward, off balance. "Are you going to be all right?" he asked. Al hacked and brought up phlegm. "Maybe you'd better take it easy tomorrow," Burney suggested. Neither of his parents said anything, and after a while he went back to bed, dizzy with the smell of eucalyptus.

Burney went out fishing by himself the next morning, when the sun was already burning off the mist. Even waking so late, he had been the only one up. He didn't bother with the motor, just rowed away from the dock a little and started casting toward shore. Rowed, cast, drifted, cast, rowed. He worked gradually out of sight of the cabin, not getting a strike, seeing nothing disturb the still surface except a family of muskrats about a mile from the cabin. The adult and two kits veered a little toward shore to avoid him, though their sleek dark heads cutting through the water showed no sign of fear. Burney sat quietly while they passed, then took up the oars again and rowed, watching the three heads until all he could see of them was the glimmer of their delicate wake.

Through the binoculars Laurel was able to distinguish the tight folds of the muskrats' minute ears, could see each feature of the adult's streamlined head mirrored in the twins, which trailed it around the end of the dock and then circled back underneath. She waited for them to reappear. When they did not, she walked down to the dock and scanned the lake. The sun was high overhead. It was time for Burney to be coming in. Mary was already starting to prepare lunch.

Al was studying something in an almanac. When he had realized that Burney was gone, when he had looked at his rods and tackle box standing in a corner of the cabin and realized that he was never going to use them again, he had started to cry. It didn't last long, and it was never very loud. Mary had held his hand and looked past him to Laurel with a kind of furious pride, acknowledgment, and anger. Afterwards Al had teased Laurel for being such a slow reader and quoted for her a statistic that amazed him.

Late in the morning a breeze began to ruffle the surface of the lake where Burney was fishing. He had reached what appeared to be the mouth of a stream, an inlet overhung with trees and brush, with a sunken island of weeds guarding the entrance. It reminded him of a spot on another lake, in another state, where he and his father had fished for sunnies when he was very little, a spot so reliable that they always referred to it as the butcher shop. He didn't much like to still-fish anymore. He didn't have the patience. It might be fun with a kid, though. Those sunnies had been like big slabs of gold. He peered down into the clear, peat-tinted water, wishing he had a can of worms with him. The sun glinted up at him. It was time to go in.

He was drifting with the wind now past the mouth of the stream, and he began to cast, knowing that it was time to go in, riffles or no riffles. Already the cabin would be filled with the old fragrance of frying onions and potatoes and simmering Polish sausages. It was time to go in. He drifted a little past the inlet, casting back as close as he dared to the branches of an overhanging willow. That was where they would be, where a stream flowed into the lake, where insects would drop in the water.

The Birthday Present

For a long time, it seemed like a mistake. Not her one-night stand with a linguist from Berkeley at the Modern Language Association convention. Not even her telling me about it in a tearful Sunday morning of confession two months later. She is a scholar, an expert on Renaissance poetry, and she knows the power of particulars, but giving me the details was not the mistake.

"What did you do?" I asked her after a long silence, staring up at the familiar, mysterious water marks on the bedroom ceiling. I could hear our five-year-old boy downstairs in the family room, playing air hockey with a neighbor kid, and I wondered if he had eaten any breakfast. It had been over a year since Mike learned to leave us alone on Sunday mornings in exchange for eating lunch out at some hamburger or pizza place.

"What do you mean?" she asked, wiping her nose. "What have I been doing here – talking about the weather?"

"I mean what, exactly, did you do with him? Exactly. I want to know." I wasn't at all sure that I wanted to know.

"What does it matter? It meant nothing. He had absolutely no significance in my life. I told you that. I was just bored. I'd been feeling sort of neglected. I felt flattered by his interest. It just happened. It'll never, never happen again. I never want to feel this horrible again, ever."

"Okay," I said. "Okay, I believe you."

"Thank God."

"But I still need to know. It'll drive me crazy otherwise, guessing."

She turned onto her back and lay still. Finally she said, "I went down on him. We pawed each other a little. I blew him. Then I went back to my room. We didn't even talk the next day."

"Well," I said. The image of her bent over faceless him was churning inside me, not quite unpleasantly, as when you've just thrown up. "Well."

"So what happens now?" she asked. "What do we do? How do we deal with this?"

There was a crash. I pulled on a robe and went downstairs and found that one of the boys had flipped the puck into my model-railroad display case, smashing a glass door.

I said, "Go outside."

"But, Dad – "

"Get out. Now. We'll talk later."

When I got back upstairs, she had put on her robe and was sitting on the edge of the bed, her bare feet looking a little blue against the white carpet. I sat beside her.

"What do you want to do?" she asked. "What do you want me to do?"

"I believe you when you say it won't happen again," I began. "I believe everything you say. But I can't just let it go. I could say that I did, but it would always be eating on me, and I'd end up hating you."

"So what do you want? I can't undo it. You want to hit me, go ahead. But you're not the hitting type."

I did want to hit her, then, for the edge of contempt I heard in her voice. But she was right: I'm not the hitting type. I said, "I want you to do for me what you did for him." She gave a crazy, relieved laugh. "Wait," I said. "I want you to do it on your birthday, every year on your birthday." Even as I was saying it, it seemed like a mistake, and it would seem like a mistake for a long time. She looked at me with an unreadable expression on her face, then slowly nodded. I dressed and went downstairs to check the damage to my trains.

Her birthday was several weeks after the confession. I bought her an especially expensive bracelet, which she seemed to appreciate, and that night she slid down in bed without my saying anything about it.

"Tell me," I said after a while. "Did you go to MLA thinking something like that would happen?"

She stopped moving, then continued until I came. She left the room, came back, and lay down beside me. "I wasn't thinking about anything," she said, "except getting away from holiday bullshit for a few days, maybe seeing a play, and finding a decent replacement for poor old Ruth Jordan."

"I remember my last MLA," I said, "flying all the way to San Francisco for an interview with the only school in the country looking for a Romanticist. By the time I saw them, they were all half-potted and just went on and on about the silk wallpaper on the bathroom ceiling."

"You're well out of that," she said. "Haven't you been a lot happier, working for the state, having the rest of your time for yourself, no paper grading?"

"Poor old Ruth Jordan – she was in linguistics?"

"Eighteenth century." She spoke coolly, without hesitation. This was a part of it, she seemed to think. "Look," she said, "I didn't plan anything, and he had nothing to do with anything else. I didn't have my diaphragm with me. That's why I blew him. To get it over with."

"It'll never be over," I said. "It'll never be over for us."

We had a pretty good year after that. My son started school, my wife got tenure at the university, and I was transferred to a division where I had more responsibility and independence. Our sex life was pretty good, too. She was a little distant for a while, but then things got back to normal. From time to time she went down on me and I on her, as we had before, and as before we were generally quite conventional about sex. Comfortable, perhaps, is the word. Maybe there hadn't been a mistake.

When her next birthday approached, however, and I asked her what sort of gift she wanted, she told me it wasn't her birthday and she had everything she needed. I bought her some nice earrings, anyway, and went with Mike to help pick out a scarf or perfume or something. After supper, Mike asked why she had not baked the usual cake and how we could have a birthday without candles and when would we sing. She told him it was not her birthday. She thanked him for his present, opened it, and thanked him again. She said she would open my present when it was her birthday. I found it that night on my dresser, where she usually put loose change that fell out of my trousers. It was unopened.

"Cute," I said, when we got into bed. "A little cruel on the kid, but cute."

She said, "I don't know what you're talking about. Wasn't that nice of him to give me a present? Well, good night, honey."

I lay there for a long time, trying to think what to say, then trying merely to figure out what I felt, succeeding in neither effort. The following year, I asked her, "Well, are you going to pull that same routine about your birthday?"

She said, "It was no routine."

"I thought we had an agreement. This seems like just another kind of cheating. Maybe this is what I should have expected."

" 'Cheating,' " she said. "I never cheated. I went to bed once with another man, and I wish to God that I hadn't, but I never cheated."

"Okay, call it what you want. But we had an agreement, a little reminder for your birthday. If you've changed your mind, why don't you just say so?"

"I haven't changed my mind. I just don't have birthdays anymore."

I laughed, partly out of surprise, partly out of a kind of bitter helplessness that I'd never experienced before. "Fine," I said. "You want to explain that to Mike? I don't give a damn, but what's he supposed to think?"

She went to the back door and called out, "Mike! Come in here a minute."

He came running from the garage driveway, where he had been trying to shoot baskets.

"Mike," she said, "I just wanted to let you know something, so you won't be confused. I'm not having birthdays anymore, so you don't have to worry about a present."

"How does that work? How can somebody not have a birthday?"

"It just happens sometimes."

He thought for a minute, bouncing the basketball every once in a while on the kitchen floor, until I told him to stop. "How about Mother's Day?"

"That's still on," she said. "Also Christmas and Valentine's Day and everything else."

"All right," he said. "I still get one, don't I?"

"Sure."

He looked over at me. "How about Dad?"

She said, "Oh yes."

"You want me for anything else?" he asked and then dribbled unsuccessfully down the back stairs, retrieved the ball from a flower bed, and returned to his solitary game against the garage.

When he was gone, I said, "I really think you've gone crazy."

"Maybe," she said.

I said, "Listen, let's just forget all this. I want us to get back to normal."

"Are you saying you were wrong to impose a penance on me?"

I listened to the intermittent dull rattle of Mike's basketball against the flimsy backboard and hoop. "Okay," I said, "maybe I was wrong. Let's just put the whole business behind us."

"I don't believe you can do that," she said.

"I can try. We can try."

"Well," she said, "good luck."

She still refused presents on her birthday, however, and let the candles burn down into the frosting on the cake I had made. She and Mike giggled as if it were all a big joke.

When I turned forty, she threw a surprise "over the hill" party for me, with all the paraphernalia – black balloons, black crepe-paper bunting, black ribbons and wrapping paper on gag gifts, gag cards, licorice jelly beans – that had somehow become a fad. It was all as corny and overdone as possible. I took it in good spirit, however, as you have to, that being the whole point. At the height of the silliness, it occurred to me that there was an answer here to my other problem, a way to break through the pearl-smooth stubbornness that she had thrown around my meanness.

I waited two years, biding my time, settling into a middle age that the joke mourning and insults of the party were intended to defuse. For the first time in my life, I started to put on weight. My hairline drifted back inexorably, and my father began to creep into my mannerisms and my mirror. I bided my time, endured it, and sent out secret party invitations to an ambush on my wife's approaching fortieth birthday.

The day of the party, I called in sick, to put up decorations and clean house and cook. It was raining in the morning and getting colder, and by late afternoon one of our March blizzards had closed many roads and made some freeway ramps impassible. After her graduate seminar that evening, my wife called from the university to tell me that she hadn't been able to get her car started and was going to spend the night in the apartment of a colleague who lived near campus.

"I wish you could make it," I said.

"No hope, babe. Give Mike a kiss for me."

"He's staying overnight with Rick Simms."

"Okay," she said. "Got to go. Rachel's leaving now."

By the time I hung up, the doorbell was ringing – some of our neighbors were starting to straggle in. Friends who had four-wheel drive made it too, smug and self-satisfied, and brought with them other, less provident couples. And so we had the party anyway and toasted my wife in absentia. "She can't really be forty," people kept saying all evening. "Was she one of your students?" they asked me. "You dirty old man!" A woman said, "I'd give anything to have her genes," and her husband muttered, ". . . get into her jeans."

The male stripper who had been hired for the event by some of my wife's women friends somehow made it through the storm and exactly fit the tone of ribaldry that was taking over the party. He had brought his own records and stripped from mittens, parka, and Sorel boots down to a leopard brief, then danced with the women and our one gay friend. He turned out to be a nice kid, and everyone was sorry to see him go when he finally dressed and struggled out into the night. He had to study, he said. He couldn't count on classes being canceled the next day.

As I danced later on with a woman who lived across the street, I thought about having an affair myself, evening things up, canceling out the whole damn birthday thing. But the woman I was dancing with wouldn't be the one. She was hot enough just then, revved up by the jokes and the stripper, but I had watched her shuffling around her house when she thought nobody could see in their big picture window, looking plain as a stone or chewing out her husband or screaming at the kids. She pressed up against me – a nice rounded woman, I'll give her that – and I thought, *No, it'd have to be a stranger*, but I went out less and less willingly. I thought of my wife's hard runner's calves and thighs and small high breasts, and my neighbor sighed against my throat, misunderstanding.

When the front door shut on the last guest, I watched the snow drive and eddy for a few minutes before I turned off the porch light and faced the debris of the party. I thought, *The stripper might have been one of my wife's students*. Maybe it was the constant contact with college kids that kept her youthful, though the little whiners had seemed to heap age on me like flowers on a casket. I dumped ashtrays, loaded the dishwasher, and wrapped leftover food and crammed it into the refrigerator. *Age buried me,* I thought, *thickened my belly and jowls.*

I found one more ashtray on the mantel, tossed the heap of butts into the fireplace, and stood there, holding the shallow soapstone bowl. I pressed my tongue into the cold hollow, rough with ash and tar, and licked until the polished green surface gleamed.

The sad and violent taste lingered in my mouth for weeks, but when it was gone, it left behind an unexpected sweetness. Years later my wife said to me, out of the blue, "You know, I'm starting to feel a birthday coming on."

I didn't know what to say. "What prompts this?" I finally asked.

"Age." I knew that she meant my age, not hers. "I want you to be able to enjoy it."

"I'll be able," I said. "Don't worry about me."

"Anyway," she said, "it's about time. I wouldn't like us to be too far apart."

"Don't worry about me," I said again, thinking how lucky I'd been, growing old with this lovely ageless woman, that one error lying between us like a golden ring.

There must have been something panicky in my voice, because she said, "There, don't worry. We have a few surprises for each other yet."

"I'm not sure that I do."

"I saw you with your old Romantics anthology the other day. That was a surprise."

"I was trying to remember a poem by John Clare that I thought Mike would like. 'Badger.' "

"Did he?"

"He liked it when the badger was winning, beating all the dogs, biting the drunks that were baiting him. It made him angry when they kill him at the end. He couldn't believe that people used to do that sort of thing."

I went and got the book, a graduate-school text I'd never

had a chance to teach from – underlined, margins crowded with comment – and turned back to Clare. "Listen to this opening: 'When midnight comes a host of dogs and men / Go out and track the badger to his den, / And put the sack within the hole, and lie / Till the old grunting badger passes by.' I love that, 'the old grunting badger.' "

She took the book, read the poem, and glanced at some others. " 'Little Trotty Wagtail'? 'Clock-a-Clay'?"

"He was mad as a coot most of the time," I said. "Actually, 'Clock-a-Clay' is pretty good. It's like a song from Shakespeare."

She looked at me skeptically, read the poem, turned the page. "Here's a good one," she said. " 'Black absence hides upon the past, / I quite forget thy face . . .' "

I said, "All he can finally remember is her name and dark hair and eyelashes. It's very convincing."

She read from another: " 'I lost the love of heaven above, / I spurned the lust of earth below . . .' That's like Blake, isn't it?" she said.

I took the book from her and closed it. "You know," I said, "I'm not sure anymore when your birthday is."

She said, "I'll let you know."

The Best Thing in the World

OUTSIDE THE MUSIC AND typewriter shop, Burney Nichols hesitated, calculating how much time he had before picking up his two-year-old from day care. He could see that there were no customers in the shop, half a floor below street level, where Sid Grosz sat on a stool reading something. In an hour he had to be at the day care, a ten-minute bike ride away. He needed to get a new A-string. In other words, it would be close, but he really needed the string and hadn't talked to Sid in a while, anyway. So he locked his bike to a parking meter, stepped down into the dark shop crowded with old typewriters, violins, banjos, guitars, and the parts and equipment needed to repair them.

"I missed ya!" Sid roared, once he recognized who it was. He was a tall, magnificent-looking man, with a mass of white hair that rose in waves from his high forehead, sweeping back, spreading over his frayed shirt collar. "I thought you was mad at me!" Sid talked so loud that people assumed he was deaf. At eighty-nine he had a right to be, but in fact his hearing was perfect. He just talked loud. His eyes had been giving him trouble, however. "What the hell do you call that stuff that films up your whatchamacallits?"

"Cataracts."

"Right!" They had made him stop driving. They wouldn't even let him ride his old one-lung Triumph, so now he got around on a Raleigh three-speed that he kept always in high gear. "Riding a bike's the best thing in the world for you! What could be better for you? Nothing could be! Listen," Sid roared, "you think that's right?"

"Sure. It's great."

"Why is that? Why is it good for you?"

"Well, I don't know – exercise keeps the heart strong, keeps the blood moving, tones your muscles – that sort of thing."

"Let me ask you something." Sid leaned across the ancient glass display counter as if speaking in confidence, though anyone passing by outside could have heard him. "A fellow told me riding a bicycle is good for the bowels! You believe that?"

"Sure. I guess so. Sure."

Sid slapped the rippled glass of the counter top. "You said it! Best thing in the world to keep you from binding up – you know what I mean? You want to know what my doctor told me last month? One of the finest doctors in town! Has an office right downtown here! A fine location! He told me it looked like I'd live forever!" He laughed thunderously. "He's crazy, though! Another thing – he wants me to have that worst eye operated on! You think I should?"

"He's the doctor. It's your eye."

"I'll tell you something," Sid said. "After I came out of his office, I talked to one of the girls. The top girl they got working there! What do you call them?"

"Nurse? Assistant? Receptionist?"

"That's it! And I asked her if she thought I should wait, if it would hurt anything to wait, make it any worse, and she said no, it wouldn't hurt at all! The top girl! You believe that, that it wouldn't hurt anything if I waited awhile? Maybe it'd get better by itself if I kept in top shape!"

"Cut it out, Sid. You always ask me this medical stuff. I don't know anything about it."

"The hell you don't!" Sid boomed, as if his leg had been outrageously pulled. "You know a hell of a lot! Since you fixed my bike, it runs like a million bucks!"

"Seat feel any better since we tilted it that way?"

"Seat feels great! Doesn't pinch me in the testes no more! Listen, riding a bike is the best thing in the world for you, right? You love it, right?"

"Sure."

"You sure do! Of course you do! Now let me ask you something! Riding a bike helps every part of your body, right? Helps all your muscles?"

"Right."

"So the eye's a muscle, right?"

"Wait – no, it's got muscles attached to it, but it isn't a muscle itself."

"It's not a muscle? What is it?"

"Well, it's an organ, I guess."

"What's an organ?"

"I can't explain it. A bunch of tissue that does something special."

"Well, doesn't exercise help organs, same as muscles?"

"Probably, sure. Gets more blood to them."

"Okay, so do you think if I rode this bike every day, maybe two hours a day, my eye might get better?"

"Come on, Sid. I don't know."

"What the hell you come in for, then, if you won't give me some free advice?"

"I need a new A-string."

A bell over the door made a brief commotion, and a woman came in lugging a typewriter for repair. While Sid waited on her, explaining at the effortless top of his voice everything he'd do to it, and how he thought a business should be run, and what this part of Minneapolis had been like fifty years ago when he'd opened the shop, and about his playing guitar in Eddie Hendrickson's orchestra in the thirties, and how he'd gotten into the typewriter and music business, and what the doctor had said about how long he would live, and what the top girl had said, Burney wandered back to the orderly workbench, where a violin lay in about twenty pieces.

Burney didn't want to get involved in a typewriter conversation just now – and not only because he didn't have much time. He had recently ordered a word processor and felt anxious about it. Sid Grosz had a violent prejudice against all computers, and mention of word processors sent him into arias of disgust. Someday Burney might have to own up to his betrayal of good counsel, but, on the other hand, eighty-nine was eighty-nine.

He examined the used violins for sale, wondering how much he'd have to pay for a better one than what he'd bought a few years ago from Sid, when he'd decided to learn to play. The violin he had was old but nameless. It had a fine tone but looked beat up.

The customer left, and Sid came back to the workbench. "Look at that mess!" he shouted. "You know what they said happened to it? They said one of their kids stepped on it! You believe that?"

"You got an A-string, Sid? I have to get going." The big schoolroom clock above the bench showed that he was already late.

"Aw," Sid boomed, "I talk too damn much. I'm boring you, ain't I?"

"Of course not – I just have to pick up my kid."

"What'd you say you wanted?" Sid seemed a little chastened.

"A-string. Broke it yesterday."

"How'd you break it? Didn't we smooth out the groove in the whatchamacallit good enough? Thing at the top?"

"Nut? I don't know. I'll look at it again before I put the new string on."

"You must play that damn fiddle all the time, right?"

"As much as I can. Been pretty busy."

"You love that fiddle, don't you? A violin is the best thing in the world – am I right? Nobody's ever figured out a better way to make them in hundreds of years, ever since what's-his-name? Italian guy?"

"Stradivarius."

"You love that fiddle, don't you? You love it!"

"You found me a beauty, Sid."

"Remember how I worked the whole damn night that time, figuring out where that buzz was coming from? You remember where it finally was?"

"Right under the bridge, where nobody could see it."

"*Nobody* could see it! How could they see it under the bridge? But we got it, right? You must play that fiddle all the time, you love it so much."

Burney glanced up at the clock again, and Sid hustled heavily toward the tall oak-framed glass case where he kept violin parts. "I should never've kept you so long! You should tell me to shut up! Now you're going to get your butt kicked!"

"It's fine, Sid. I'll make it."

Sid rummaged slowly through a box of small square envelopes and finally found what he was looking for.

"What do you get for this, Sid?"

"From you, nothing!"

"Come on." Sid rarely charged him for anything except major purchases. Usually he wouldn't even let him pay cost. "Cost, at least, Sid. I put you out of business, where will I go then?"

"You get out of here! Get your little girl before she kills you! I should pay you for coming in – you're like an encyclopedia for me!" As Burney left, Sid roared at him, "Bring that fiddle in sometime! We'll play duets!"

"You bet!" Burney's timing was so bad he couldn't play with anyone, not even his teacher. "That'll be great!"

After supper Burney tried to put in the new string while Greta, his little girl, whined for him to go out, go for a walk with her, let her "see the guys," which was what she called the gang of kids, one of them no older than she was, who dodged in and out of traffic all evening.

"No play your violin," she ordered, at first in an adult's reasonable voice, then escalating to a scream. "No play your violin!" She leaned hard into his leg, clutching under her arm the threadbare, snot-crusted stuffed toy dog that had been her constant companion ever since she learned to walk.

"*No play your violin!*" When she was a baby, her face would start collapsing at the first note he played, and a half-verse of "Twinkle, Twinkle, Little Star" would have her howling. It was better now, though she still wasn't crazy about it. "*No play your violin! No play your violin!*"

"I'm not going to play. I'm trying to fix it."

"Fick it later. No fick it now."

With difficulty he managed to remove the tangled old stub of string from the mortised head and threaded the new string into the hole of the peg. Although the little girl's nagging, weeping, nerve-wracking complaints grew louder, he was resolved to finish this job, if no other, and to do it in one sitting.

While he was trying to coax the eyelet end into its slot in the tailpiece, the little girl suddenly reached up and slammed her dog across the belly of the violin, knocking the bridge ajar and snapping something else.

"Damn it!" he shouted and grabbed the dog from her and hurled it out the door into the living room.

Outraged, she instantly charged him, screaming, "You naughty boy," pummeling him on the knee with clenched fists like a battering of crab apples. She raced for the dog, hugged it with a passion that would haunt him for days, and clambered, sobbing, up the stairs in search of her mother.

He made love with her mother later that night. They were trying to make a second baby and, having had no success after several months, had decided to try intercourse every night during what might be her fertile period. This was the fifteenth straight night, and both Burney and Laurel found themselves drawing rather more deeply than usual on the resources of imagination. He had once fantasized about inevitable sex, but this was not quite the same.

After making love, Laurel would go through a sort of yoga routine in bed, lying in a series of peculiar positions, some distinctly uncomfortable, intended to make gravity assist in what levity and the life force had begun. Burney was under severe orders not to fall asleep during this appendix and leave her poised, propped up like some kind of ninny, alone. Often during this time, their talk turned to Greta, whose richly cherished autocracy they had been sweating to subvert.

"What happened to get her so worked up tonight?" Laurel asked. "I thought you were going to keep her occupied so I could get that report done."

He told her, stressing the head cold and a possible ear infection that were making the kid even more demanding and short-tempered and unreasonable than usual. "Where did she get that 'naughty boy' stuff, do you suppose?" he asked.

"I don't know. Day care, I guess. Robby."

"Poor Robby." They talked for a while, in sympathetic yet self-satisfied terms, about one of Greta's day-care brothers, a boy only a month older than her two and a half years but taller, heavier, and stronger than most four-year-olds. "People expect too much when a kid's big for his age," Burney said. "He still wants to be cuddled and picked up, and he weighs – what? Fifty pounds?"

"Maybe that's what makes some big kids turn into bullies. They don't get held enough."

"Every bully I knew was just about my size." This was not true, but he had found that contention made it easier to stay awake.

"Well, there you are."

"What's that supposed to mean?"

"I don't know. I was just teasing. Joke."

"I'm about as far from a bully as anybody I ever knew."

"Sure, honey. Skip it. I'm bushed, and I'm going to have to get up early to finish that report." She rolled over then onto her stomach – a part of the routine that never made sense to him.

Instead of companionably rolling over too, he lay staring at the ceiling. "I'm a wimp, if anything."

She laughed, muffled by the pillow. "Sure," she said. "You're a regular sissy. If we were at the beach right now, I'd kick sand in your face." Finally she settled into her usual fetal tuck, wrapped around a pillow.

He turned toward her after a while. "You weren't thinking about that thing with Greta's mutt, were you?" She didn't answer. Usually, despite orders and his best intentions, he drifted off before her, but now he lay wide-awake, restless and lonely. He got up, pulled on a robe, and fumbled in the dark for his slippers. The little girl, probably, had carried them off somewhere, though he was pretty careless with them himself. He felt in all the usual places where she liked to put things – between the mattress and the footboard, inside the humidifier, behind the curtains, under a pile of toys that had drifted up against the side of Laurel's dresser. At last he gave up – it was a warm night anyway – and went downstairs barefoot, the buckling shrunken floorboards unexpectedly precarious underfoot.

After drawing the shades in his study, he switched on a lamp, set up his music stand and music, and ran a finger lightly over the strings of the violin. The new A was already noticeably flat, even to his uncertain ear. He looked around for the heavy brass practice mute that he had to use late at night. It seemed to be nowhere. Without it, his wife and child and very likely the next-door neighbors would be torn from their beds by the sounds hc was about to produce. When he was struggling with a new piece or a new position, even he could not bear the racket and was grateful for the hushing mass of brass riding the nervous bridge, absorbing almost all the noise. Now it seemed to be nowhere, and the itch to pull his bow hard over the waiting untuned strings swelled into a kind of rage, as if nothing else would satisfy him. He plucked the flat A again, and even that brief pizzicato set the crib overhead stirring and creaking.

And so he did what he had done from time to time before getting the mute. He grabbed violin and bow dangerously in one hand, music stand and music in the other, and descended into the cool squalor of the basement. Here, standing on the damp floor beside the washer and drier, with the cat shuffling in the neglected litter box, trying to avoid its own desiccated turds, he could safely assault even the Bach *Double Concerto*, which he shouldn't have tried without at least two more years of hard work. The opening measures of the first movement, which was all that he could read, tended to go so slowly for him that it seemed utterly unrelated to the recording of the *Double* he listened to again and again, hoping to drive into his fingers and bow hand the knowledge that eluded his intermittent conscious efforts.

Rough tuning the A, he decided the other strings were close enough for playing in a basement. Then, skipping the warm-up scales and études that his teacher insisted on, he shifted his chilling feet a little and drove headlong into the black vivace of the *Double* and actually staggered through to the end of the second line before faltering to a stop.

Not bad. Not too damn bad. But by this time the decaying concrete floor was getting really uncomfortable, not only cold but also gritty with cat litter and sawdust and who knows what. There was no longer a rug down there – swelling spring ground water the year before had taken care of that – and so he dragged over the splitting, ancient comforter, beyond usefulness even as a drop cloth, on which the cat usually slept.

Slick with matted cat hair, the comforter at first was not much better than the bare concrete, but once he had adjusted to the peculiar sensation, it felt all right. He struggled through ten more measures of the Bach and then turned to the études and then even played some scales and then worked through a once-familiar set of sonatas by Corelli, the underlined passages taking new evasions. And then he went over a piece by Handel that he once had memorized for a recital, concentrating now not on the music but on maintaining a placid facial expression. Someone had giggled during the recital, and Laurel thought it might have been at his contorted forehead. He wished he had a mirror now.

He played and played, the basement beams shivering in the

rush of evilly distorted but sometimes almost actual music. He played till his left wrist and forearm ached with the twist that should have been effortless, that would have been unconscious and natural had he started thirty years before, that would be natural for Greta in a few years if she could be talked into taking the Suzuki program with him.

Finally he stopped, feeling dazzled and empty. He *did* love it, he thought. It *was* the best thing in the world, however awful it would seem to the world itself. He fed the cat and gave it fresh water. Leaving the music stand and the music in the basement, he ascended with the violin and slack bow to the fluorescent gleam of the kitchen and shuffled cautiously through the rest of the darkened downstairs, kicking toys aside from his path.

When he was almost at the stairs, something caused him to go back and look for the last toy he'd encountered. It was a plastic cement truck, and in its barrel he found the practice mute. Its soft dull surface glowed somehow invisibly, a charged talisman, its smooth bevels, mass and coolness, rounded prongs and faint engraving seeming to say to him, "Hush. Hush."

King Arthur

BECAUSE I TOOK CARE OF them, they called me Mom, though I thought of myself as King Arthur. Well, he was a kind of mother, too, worrying about his children, breaking up fights, hoping that the right seating arrangement would finally make them all happy. Encouraging goodness. A father is like Merlin – arbitrary and absent. I was their mother. I was King Arthur.

In the beginning, they took care of me. I fell out of my freshman dorm window onto a riot-armored policeman during the Cambodia protests, got cursed, Maced, billy-clubbed, and arrested. I passed out and was somehow misplaced and carried off to the house where I would live for the next ten years.

I woke, head aching, blinded, floating upon a scummy waterbed sloshing and heaving at every movement, in a darkness that was wet and stank of mildew and vomit and God knows what. When I yelled, a door opened above me. Somebody stood outlined in the doorway and told me to shut up, which I could not seem to do. Somebody pushed past him. He switched on a light that placed me suddenly in a dark-paneled basement. He came down the stairs, and crouched over me, asking me if I was all right and could I please be quiet. After a while I could.

At the time, it seemed quite possible that I would be pursued and thrown into jail, with my initial charges compounded by resisting arrest and flight from custody. As it turned out, the police and campus security guards were too worried about the protection of college property to mind demonstrators leaving, in whatever condition.

Still, when I was brought upstairs, they pulled the few shades that would stay down and asked me to keep away from windows. They settled me at the kitchen table, and somebody asked if I wanted a beer. "Yes," I said, "thanks." I almost threw up at the stench that billowed out of the refrigerator, one of two crowded into the horrible kitchen. At first I thought that my sensitivity was a reaction to the gas or the head bashing, but one of the boys, the guy who had first spoken to me, shouted for somebody to close the damn door before he got sick or something. This was Rainier, muscular, deeply tanned, handsome.

Another guy, with a long cinnamon-colored beard, laughed and said, "When you landed on that pig, I thought, 'Shit, the dormies are putting us to shame.' After that, *I* kicked a little tail, let me tell you."

A girl spoke then, half-hidden behind one of the refrigerators. "It was just about the greatest thing I've ever seen. Not *you*, Eric. I didn't see you do anything but make a lot of noise."

Eric laughed indulgently, "Lighten up, Rita."

"No," she said, "that leap out the window, taking them by surprise. That's what turned the tide. We'd never have gotten past them otherwise."

I sipped uneasily at the not very cold beer, wondering how

long it would be before I dared go back to my room. They told me that I should stay with them for a day or two, until things cooled off. I turned down their offer of the waterbed in the basement, which they regarded as their guest room, and agreed to sleep on the enormous exploding couch that took up much of the living room. I pushed a dog off it and lay down, with a chewed-up afghan for cover, and watched the room turn in great slow circles around me.

More than a dozen people were living there off and on – mostly students attending my college, some who had gone for a semester or so and then dropped out, a dishwasher from a restaurant where somebody worked, and a few people whose connections with the others never did become clear. The city owned the property and rented the house to college boys for next to nothing. Sooner or later it would be torn down to make room for some building project.

Most of the housemates had been involved in the demonstration, and the atmosphere that night became increasingly festive as other demonstrators dropped by with beer and marijuana. For hours they talked fervent politics and philosophy, and their egos seemed gradually to dissolve in boiling purpose. I lay forgotten and comfortable under the dreadful afghan and felt myself a part of something wonderful, something utterly separate from the life I had known.

I woke to the smell of a candle end guttering and smoldering on a stack of *Playboys*. Traffic murmured intermittently outside, and a dog lay snoring at the foot of the couch. In front of the burnt-out fireplace, somebody was sleeping wrapped in the flag that had been draped over a hole where charred wall studs stood naked. I extinguished the candle, turned out some lights, and went into the kitchen for a drink of water. It took me over an hour to wash the dishes piled in crusted, moldy stacks overflowing from the sink onto the counter top and stove. After I had rearranged the cupboards to hold everything, I took a deep breath and attacked the worse of the two refrigerators, working gradually back to the ripest and most ancient bowls of food, corroded cartons of milk curds, and festering unopened packages of pork chops and hamburger, weeks beyond expiration. I found a garbage bag, filled it, and hauled it through the unmown weeds of the yard to the alley. I felt so grateful.

At the end of the term, I moved in for good, taking over a bedroom from a guy who had graduated and gone back to Colorado. When I pushed the bed into the center of the room to paint over the nicotine-bronzed nursery wallpaper – bears, clowns, and toy soldiers on a field of what once must have been pale green – I discovered yellowing stains trailing down onto the baseboard, which made me question his reputation for sexual conquest. It was none of my business, however, and I resisted the temptation to draw others' attention to the evidence. Anyway, paint covered it all: childhood and poison and passion splattered against a secret wall.

I cleaned the smoke sludge off the inside of the window and crawled out onto the porch roof to wash the outside. Neighborhood kids playing in the street shouted up to me, and their mothers watched me in surprise. The window trim was a little rotten, shedding its paint in long scales. I thought about painting and bought scraper, brush, and paint, but before two windows were finished, a greater idea seized me, a thought curved and unifying.

"You're kidding," Rainier said when I had explained things to him. "Why a rainbow?"

"Because it would be beautiful," I said. I'd lay it out, and we all could work on it. I had begun working a summer job in a metalwork factory by then, running a hoist that dipped mobile-home steps and handrails into hot stripper, then into a huge vat of black paint, before hooking them onto an endless conveyer chain to dry and be stacked. Color was about all I had on my mind. A rainbow was color.

Nobody seemed to mind, though neither was there much enthusiasm for the project at first. Rainier would start law school in the fall, and he was devoting the summer to hanging out at Lake Calhoun, pretending to read the thickest of his new textbooks. He pitched in for paint, though, and

Richard, a biology major two years ahead of me, and Sarah, his girlfriend, helped me pencil concentric arcs on the clapboard of the house beneath the front-porch roof, using string and a nail driven into the threshold for a compass.

David, the dishwasher, was working nights then, but he got up early and helped me start the painting on a Saturday morning. By noon the porch was crowded with housemates dabbing and jabbing brushes in a dozen styles, yet staying within the lines and respecting the order of the spectrum I had posted on a sheet of paper and had painted as samples into the top of each arc, from crimson on the outside down to the deepest purple we could find for the tight inner arc. Some of these people were still half-wasted from Friday-night parties, and a few of them hadn't taken instructions seriously in years. That's why they were living there, to get away from anybody who would tell them what to do. Nevertheless, they worked together. They stayed within the lines.

We stalled for a while over the question of what to do where the picture window and the front door interrupted the rainbow. We finally decided to go right over them, painting over the glass, using Sarah's diamond ring tied to our compass string to scribe the arcs, and doing the doorway three times – on the outside and the inside of the storm door and on the outside of the main door, so that no matter how the doors stood, the rainbow was continuous.

Neighbors passed by all day, watching the progress – not so much the other renters on the block but the home owners, who had grown suspicious of the house during years of drunken parties and drug traffic. As many as nine squad cars at once had responded to calls during some of the more spectacular parties in the past, and the neighbor across the street told me of sitting on his porch all night with a loaded shotgun after somebody from the house tried to kick his door in, too drunk to know where he lived. Well, I thought, this rainbow will be a sign visible to even the blindest drunk: *Come in – this is your place.*

To some of the neighbors, the rainbow was appalling, just

the sort of hippie gesture they expected from us, thwarting their efforts to turn the neighborhood back to residential, single-family, property-owning respectability. When I saw them passing by with that look on their faces, I'd wave and put down my brush and encourage them to come over and celebrate when it was done. "I'm Art," I'd say. "You live in the green house don't you? I know that little one. He rides his trike all day long, doesn't he! So what do you think? How do you like it?"

And they would laugh, embarrassed by their ungenerous thoughts, and say, "It's sure different! But, no, I kind of like it." And their kid would shout, "I love it! It's so pretty I want to paint one on *my* house!" The kid's parents would laugh and say, "Well, maybe sometime," meaning the weekend after hell freezes over. But many of them did come over that evening and have a beer or a glass of lemonade, and one old guy, who admitted to me that he had been lobbying the city for years to tear down the house, came over with a big bag of popcorn his wife had made for us, and we all had a great time.

There was paint left over when we had finished, mainly from the lower end of the spectrum – purple, blue, dark green – and as the evening wore on, some ad hoc painting erupted, while I was inside preparing snacks. They left the rainbow alone but splotched the white pillars of the porch till they seemed eaten away by the night. I gradually got control of the paint and brushes and buried them unobtrusively in the garbage cans I'd placed at the bottom of the porch steps.

Sunday morning, before my run, I went out with a can of white and painted over the defaced pillars. By daylight, some of the rainbow's deficiencies, which had been invisible in the yellow porch light, were pretty obvious: gaps in the shadows of the clapboards, colors swerving out of line here and there, plenty of drips. After I'd repainted the pillars, I thought about correcting them. From the street, though, it looked fine, and those imperfections became a part of the design, like the deep colors that would gradually bleed through the white latex on the pillars. Over the years, I came to accept them as part of the deal.

The rainbow soon became a landmark. People would give directions by it: "Go a block past that rainbow house, then turn left." And Martha, the crone who wandered the neighborhood every day lugging a huge Persian cat, raved about the beauty of the thing till we were all sick of hearing her go on about it, and then she contented herself with just waving her hand slowly across it whenever she stopped by for coffee or iced tea. "My boys," she would say. "Thank you, thank you, thank you." We were always her boys. She pretty much ignored the girls who hung around the house, even those who practically lived there. "What would I do without my boys?" she'd say. "What would I do without my boys?"

During lunch break on Monday, I told Lucas, one of the welders, about painting the rainbow. He said, "I often wonder about the rainbow that appears when you heat steel."

"It shows what sort of temper there is, doesn't it? How hard or soft the steel is getting?"

"Sure," he said. "That's what it shows. But I wonder how it works, what makes it look like that."

"Well," I said, "let's see. Colors are caused by different wavelengths of light. When steel is heated to different temperatures, it must give off different wavelengths of light, which makes colors."

Lucas nodded and thought about it for a while. We were sitting on some pallets behind the factory, where everybody ate his lunch during nice weather. The lunchroom, though apart from the machines, carried the same reek of oil and solvents and paint that pervaded the rest of the building. "Okay," he said, "but how can it stay that color after the metal cools?" I didn't know. "I'll tell you something else," he said, crushing his sandwich wrappers and adjusting the folds of his trousers where they disappeared into his high leather boots. "You can file that color right off. It doesn't run through the metal, even if the inside was just about as hot as the outside." I didn't know why that was, either.

Lucas and Roger, the other welder, were the aristocrats of the shop. Not just because they were more skilled than the workers who ran the machines stamping out stair treads, bearing rings, dome-light brackets, or whatever else we had a contract for, responsible mainly for getting the press turned off quickly if something went wrong, before it jammed and broke the die. The welders worked at their own pace, roamed their areas, talked a lot. They also dressed differently. Even without their great masks and gauntleted gloves, they stood out. It had something to do with the thickness of their shirts, the breadth of their leather belts, the way they carried themselves. I would stand high on my platform above the tanks of stripper and paint and watch them bend into their shower of blue sparks, and I would feel proud of them, as if they were doing some true and brave thing for me.

If Lucas and Roger were aristocrats, then Rudolph Binger, the tool maker – what was he? Not royalty, though I was about to say that – one so dark of mood that he seemed almost invisible, nothing there but the pride of his skill. He never ate with the rest of us, always drove off somewhere at noon and returned a few minutes to one. While I was trying to organize a Fourth of July picnic, I went into his shop and was examining his lathes and grinders, drill presses, drawers of calipers and drafting tools, when he walked in and spoke the first English I'd ever heard from him (he communicated with the boss in German), telling me to get out. I told him about the picnic. He didn't even bother saying no. He just turned his back and began an inventory, I think, of his tools. He was a sort of wizard, I suppose, but with no tolerance for flash or society, no desire to amaze – more like a captured gnome, alien, laboring in secret, wanting no further part in even the fairest kingdom.

I got one of my housemates a job at the factory later that summer, and he said Binger was probably a Nazi and wouldn't talk to me because I was a Jew.

"But I'm not a Jew," I said.

"You're not?" Steve said. "I thought you were."

"I'm Catholic."

"Well," he said, "Binger probably thought you were Jewish."

Steve was always making that sort of judgment. This girl

was a whore, that one was frigid or lesbian. This teacher was a fascist, that one would understand no matter what, would be great to take out to a bar. He constructed great effigies, however, and when the Child Molester was going to visit our campus, we all stayed up late helping him.

Though Steve preferred to work from life, in this case he had to rely on a picture I'd cut out of *Time*, the little photograph that accompanied the Molester's newspaper column, and a cartoon that somebody had found in *Playboy*, in which the conservative columnist's jowly, judgmental face stared disapprovingly through a window at a couple in bed.

Campus radicals had howled with outraged delight when it was announced that Tom Calvin, '54, had been invited to speak at Founder's Day. Not just because he represented what they loathed most dearly – anticommunism, prescriptive morality, laissez-faire economics – but because they had what they considered the goods on him. *The Berkeley Barb* had published an article charging that Calvin had been arrested once for exposing himself to a twelve-year-old girl. It had been a long time ago, and no mainline newspaper had picked up on the story, but for us it was like a gift, a blessing.

While Steve molded the papier-mâché mask of the face, we stuffed old gloves for hands, balled up newspapers to fill out the capacious three-piece suit that had once belonged to Rainier's father, and argued about the zucchini Steve was planning to have protrude from the effigy's fly.

"Stem end or blossom end," Richard kept saying, "which seems more convincing?"

"I think you should skip it," I said. It was really a very nice veggie, one of the little ones that are so hard to find in the fall, and I had congratulated myself on buying a dozen of them at our nearby Red Owl.

"Stem end gives more of a foreskin effect," Richard said. "What do you think, Steve? Anybody know whether Calvin's circumcised or not?"

During the debate that followed, I got up and made a bunch of sandwiches from leftover turkey. When I passed them around, Kent, Richard's brother, the only freshman in the house, said, "Thanks, Mom," sort of automatically, and then laughed in embarrassment when Rainier hooted at him.

"Great sandwiches, Mom," somebody said, and somebody else said, "Yeah, Mom, can I have more milk, please?"

"*May* I," I corrected. It was a big joke for a while, mostly at Kent's expense, though partly at mine. After a few days, the joke lost its edge, and I found that I had been renamed. It's strange in my ears now, with everyone scattered, everything forgotten: "Mom."

They voted, and circumcised won. "I'm glad it's a little one," Steve said, when it was in place. "Any smaller, though, nobody would notice it."

I said, "Look, you really can't bring it that way into the field house. It's obscene. You could get arrested. They'll take it away, in any case. It'll all go to waste." This argument went on a long time. Finally I convinced Steve to safety-pin the dummy's hands over the zucchini. The result, of course, was far more obscene, much more expressive and perverted. I wished I had kept out of it.

Calvin's speech was predictable – bedrock conservative, high-toned, ironic, more witty than we liked to admit – and the hoisting of the effigy halfway through received the mixed chorus of cheers and boos that we'd come to expect. Calvin ignored the effigy, even when it was danced through the aisles and out the side door, to be burned in the usual spot on the parking lot, but when the editor of the school newspaper asked him at the interview later on, "Why did you think that little girl was interested in seeing your shriveled prick?" he went for the kid in a way that showed he'd missed nothing. Some faculty members separated them before much happened, but everyone I talked to agreed it was a satisfying conclusion.

The speech was on Friday. Sunday morning, I was running down Summit Avenue and saw somebody approaching from far off, another former jock, I assumed, or an out-of-shape basketball player trying to get ready for the season. This was 1970, and I usually had the grassy median strip to myself. I said hi when we passed. He raised one hand a little. And I thought, *That was Tom Calvin*, though it couldn't have been, running on a Sunday morning in ill-fitting sweats. He didn't even live here. He lived in California.

A block later, I decided it had been him. I jogged in place at the big intersection at Lexington, waiting for the light, crossed halfway on the green, then turned and headed back. I was in pretty good shape then, having worked hard at the factory all summer, up and down the painting platform thousands of times, and now running nearly every day since school had started again. Yet it took me a long time to catch him, the guy I thought might be Tom Calvin.

I pushed to within a block of him, then couldn't gain more than a few strides a block until he slowed for the light at Fairview. He heard me then, I think, and took off as soon as the intersection cleared and kept me half a block back for another mile. We were clearly racing then. I didn't know why. I kept thinking of the guy ahead of me as Tom Calvin, though I couldn't see how it could be. Calvin was middle-aged and paunchy, and that sort never ran on the boulevards in those days. He held back a little on the long hill down to River Road, and I kicked, flew, and sprang past him as he was looking to cross the road toward the monument overlooking the Mississippi.

I sank onto a bench and watched him approach. It *was* Calvin, breathing hard but not out of control the way I was. I expected him to say, "Good run," or something of that sort, which is what you say when you get in these impromptu races, but he just walked around the base of the monument and stood looking down at the river for a moment. He started back.

"Wait," I said. "You're Tom Calvin, aren't you?"

He turned and stood looking at me. "Yeah?" He *was* a little paunchy, but the bulldog face was misleading. I hadn't noticed at the ceremony how tall he was, and the effigy, which we'd made distinctly fat, was confusingly mixed up in who he was.

"I heard your speech the other day," I said.

He stared at me. "So what'd you think?"

It was an important moment, I knew, a chance to make the difference, to clarify the principles of freedom and humanity that the demonstration was supposed to dramatize. But before I could think of anything to say, he grunted, "Never mind. I saw you there. I know what you think. It's all so goddamned simple, isn't it?"

I said, "No, the war – "

"I was nineteen years old," he said. "I was going to be a priest. How about that? It was a real calling. I've never doubted it. And the girl was sixteen, not twelve." He paused, and I tried to say something, but he went on in a different voice. "Offering nakedness to her was . . . it was like – I don't know – a wink at God. A nudge that said, 'Okay, I get it – I see what you mean.' "

And I kept thinking, *How am I going to make my people believe this?*

"Like you get blown to kingdom come, and you say, 'I see your point – *that's* how it is.' "

"But – "

"Which is what you self-righteous little jerks never will understand. What the law means. Sin. Grace. You make me want to puke." Then he was running again, across River Road, digging into the hill as if *it* made him want to puke, the flattened grass his worst enemy, and by the time I stood up, he was almost out of sight over the hill's crest, and I hadn't even caught my breath.

The problem with being King Arthur, I thought as I walked back, is that the dragons run over you before you have a chance to draw your sword. And then you find you never had a sword anyway. You didn't pull it out of the stone – that was only a dream.

So it was no Camelot, but we lived in the house in relative peace. None of us was drafted. Nobody grew up for years and years. None of us got married. David, who was gay, moved into the big bedroom with Ted, a lawyer Rainier had met during a clinical, and I fell in love with Monica, Kent's girlfriend, who took off for Hawaii as soon as she graduated.

We made improvements – insulated the attic, caulked windows, lanced the waterbed and hauled its stinking carcass into the sun. I planted a garden, and from June to September Martha never went away without a sack of fresh vegetables or some flowers.

We cleaned the place up, yet it was only afterward that the rats appeared. Rainier met one in the enclosed back porch, and they both went kind of crazy – the rat burrowing itself into a bag of insulation, Rainier trying to kill it by hurling his bicycle again and again against the bag, which burst and billowed out a cloud of cellulose that covered the rat's escape.

At supper I kept wondering why there was a rat *now*. When the house was filthy, nobody had seen so much as a mouse. Steve said, "*Rats*, Mom, not *a* rat. For every rat you see, there are four or five keeping out of sight. You have a real problem here."

Rainier, who had been quiet up to this point, said, "I'll get the bastards. I'll take care of this," which surprised everyone. He had volunteered for no household task in anyone's memory. He was working for a little personal-injury firm then, making a pretty decent income, and I don't know why he was still living in the house.

He said, "Their butts are mine." He went to a hardware store down the block and bought a half-dozen enormous spring traps, which looked like comically oversize versions of the mousetraps we used to use at home. He baited them with peanut butter, hid them all over, and checked them three or four times before going to bed. The next morning, while I was making breakfast, I heard a whoop of joy from the basement, and Rainier charged upstairs carrying one of the traps, in which was clamped the dead body of a rat, its dark blood pooled at the mouth. He tossed it, trap and all, into the backyard, checked all the other traps, and sat drinking coffee and telling everybody how damn good it made him feel, what he felt when he'd first seen it, how much he wished he'd been able to be there when the trap was sprung.

"This is a whole new side of you," I said, glad to see him so happy but a little uneasy at his fervor.

"Bloody damn right," he said, in the English accent he sometimes affected when he was drunk. "I'm going to get *all* those bloody buggers! I'm the bloody *exterminator*!" Then he went out and speared the rat on an old barbecue fork, pried the trap open with his foot, and tried to make Roy, the last of the house dogs, attack the dead rat by jiggling it in front of him.

Roy ran away, and I said, "Get rid of it, for God's sake." Rainier finally carried the rat out to the garbage cans. He hosed off the bloody trap, reset it in the basement, and went around adding more peanut butter to the other traps.

"Aren't you going to work today?" I asked, and he reluctantly agreed that he'd better. On the way to his car, though, he told a neighbor all about the experience, which seemed to me a serious mistake. I never stopped worrying about the reputation of the house. But the neighbor, a retired railroad engineer, had had rats too and seemed to enjoy the story.

Briefly after that, pest control became all the rage in the neighborhood. I watched one evening when a crowd gathered around the corner of a house a few doors down, where a guy with a pellet gun was shooting at a squirrel that raced back and forth on the edge of a roof. Finally the squirrel gave a little jump, apparently hit, and fell two stories to the ground. Before anybody could reach him, he got up and limped into some bushes, from which nobody could scare him. "Bastard kept getting into my attic," the home owner explained to me when I asked him about it. "I'd've shot him with my twelve-gauge if it wasn't against the law. Hell, even that pellet gun is illegal in the city! Doesn't make much noise, though."

Rainier caught one more rat, and that was the end of it, though he kept the traps freshly baited for weeks and checked them morning and night. Something had clearly gone out of his life when he gave up and let me gather in the dusty traps.

By 1980, when the eviction order arrived and the house was posted with condemnation notices, only Steve, Rainier, and I remained from the early group. A musician named Al lived in David's old room, but we hardly ever saw him, and a couple of college kids had just moved in.

It broke my heart, the thought of leaving that old place and having it torn down to make room for a new police station. I tried to mobilize neighborhood opposition, spending several evenings going from door to door with a petition, but although quite a few signed, it was obvious that most of them would just as soon see the house go.

"They *want* the pigs next door to them," Steve sneered, sorting through his stuff and throwing out the window everything he wanted to save, except his stereo. "They're all racists around here. They want protection for when the blacks start to move in."

I didn't think that was it. I thought that if only we had finished painting the trim, if we'd gotten more involved in neighborhood activities, invited people in, shown them that we were stable citizens like them, then maybe they'd have been willing to fight to keep us there. How could they not value what we had here, if they knew?

Rainier asked, "What *did* we have? It wasn't even a commune – just an old house a bunch of guys rented and lived in for a while." I understood: he was kicking himself for missing the chance to invest in real estate back when prices and interest rates were low. He was thinking about equity. Well, so was I.

I rented a little apartment near the university, resolved finally to get my master's degree. Steve decided to sleep on my couch for a while, until he figured out what to do. Rainier bought a condo in the western suburbs, and the college kids – I don't know – I guess they moved into dorms.

The city nailed plywood over all the doors and windows, surrounded our house and the one next to it with a sloppy chain-link fence, and posted NO TRESPASSING signs everywhere. It stayed that way for almost a year. I couldn't stand driving past it, it looked so forlorn, like a castle that had been enchanted, surrounded with thorns, silent and unalive.

Then, late in spring, I got a strange, excited call from Rainier, who said that he had been talking with one of the neighbors, who worked in the city-planning office, who said that the house was coming down in a week or two. I groaned and wondered what Rainier had been doing talking with one of the old neighbors. "No," he said, "wait. This guy, Dick Quinn, from that yellow house? He told me that his wife thinks there's a great old stained-glass window in there, covered up with wallboard. She said her grandmother used to live there and remembers a semicircular stained-glass window over the built-in buffet."

"There isn't any built-in buffet."

He said, "No, not now. They tore it out when they were remodeling in the fifties, but the window is still there."

"Okay," I said. "Maybe. So?"

"So we're going to get it."

"Who?"

"Me, Dick Quinn, Eric. We're going in tonight, around ten o'clock."

"Eric?"

"He's back in town, working for Control Data. He wants to see you and Steve again. Meet us at the house. Bring any tools you have. Bring beer."

Steve and I got there a little before ten, pushed our way through a gap in the chain-link fence, and circled around behind the house, where we heard voices and the creaking of nails being pulled out of boards. We stopped. "Holy shit," Steve said. The smaller house next door, a newer expansion bungalow, was gone, its foundation gaping to the lights and sounds of passing traffic.

We turned to our house. Rainier and some others were crouched around a basement window. Somebody stood up and came toward us. "Mom! Steve!" he shouted. "Right on!" Somebody hushed him. "It's me, man, Eric! Don't you guys recognize me?"

Without his beard, he looked younger than he had ten years before. While we were giving each other complicated black-power handshakes, somebody else stepped away from the group by the house.

"Arthur!" It was Rita. We hugged. Eric shouted, "Hey, man,

they're in!" Dick Quinn was sliding himself backward through the basement window. The rest of us followed, easing the drop to the basement floor by shoving an old bookcase up against the wall as a ladder. Our flashlights swept around the old dinginess as we made our way upstairs.

A little street light filtered in around the ill-fitting plywood, but we still needed flashlights. Our old stove and one of the refrigerators were still there, and the big couch sprawled crosswise in the living room, where we'd left it when we couldn't get it through the door. I felt bad that we'd left so much trash lying around, but the city hadn't given us much notice.

We spoke in low voices, more for the strangeness of being there than for safety, until Dick called out, "Here it is. This must be where the buffet was. Let's get this wall down!" While they laid into the wallboard with hammers and crowbars, I walked through the rest of the downstairs and started up to the second floor.

"Wait," Rita said, "I don't have a light." She took my hand going up the dark stairs. We stood at the bay window in the master bedroom and looked down into the cellar hole of the house next door. "Dick says they jacked it up onto beams and rollers a few weeks ago and just pulled it off down the street in the middle of the night," she said. "It must have been really weird."

"I wish somebody had told me," I said. "I wish I could have seen it." An old workbench still stood in one corner of the basement, and there were shelves attached to the wall, filled with dozens of paint cans. In the street light, pipes glinted where they had been severed. It was as if some brutal magic had occurred.

We walked through the rest of the bedrooms, listening to the racket of hammers and splitting wood below. "So," I said, "you and Eric are still together?"

"No," she said. "Well, sort of. He followed me out to New Jersey, and I guess I kind of followed him back here."

We heard him shout from downstairs, "Cover me, Starsky.

I'm going in!" A splintering crash. "All right!" he crowed. "All *right*!"

"He's really such an asshole, isn't he?" Rita said.

"Oh, I don't know."

"He is," she said. "He's fourteen years old."

We went downstairs, passed the study door swinging a little in its broken frame, and found Rainier, Steve, and Quinn finishing off the wallboard, pulling it away with their hands. I shone my flashlight between the studs, revealing an empty arc of pressboard, into which Rainier hurled his hammer. There *had* been a window there, but it had been removed when they remodeled.

"Open up! It's the police!" Eric shouted from the kitchen. He smashed the basement door. "Come out of there, you bunch of doped-up commie perverts! Eat shit!" he screamed, and a bottle smashed against the basement floor.

"Let's get out of here," Rita said. But then Quinn noticed the double-button light switches. He scraped at one with the edge of his crowbar and announced that they were brass. While he and Rainier went around unscrewing the switch plates and prying them loose from their layers of paint, Steve went to work on the oak banister, which he said he could carve into erotic walking sticks. Rita and I sat on the sofa and talked, while the sounds of pillage shook the house like rock music from the good old days.

They used a bulldozer to take the house down. Fifty or so people were gathered outside the chain-link fence by the time the bulldozer backed down from its long trailer, circled the house, and nudged up against a corner. Children cheered, and the crowd grew. The house groaned and leaned over the machine's heavy blade, and the operator shifted into reverse and retreated. He moved against the porch, nipping out the pillars and dragging off the roof, then pushed again against a corner. The long-shabby rainbow collapsed. Plywood fell away from the picture window, and the glass split apart in smooth arcs that sailed out into the front yard and shattered.

Some kids were climbing the fence to get a better view, when the chimney started shaking apart, sending bricks leaping down the roof. I pulled the kids down and sent them back to their parents. From the sidewalk, on the other side of the splintering, collapsing house, I could hear Martha crying, "What have they done to my boys?" I moved through the crowd to comfort her, but she didn't recognize me. She just stared at the falling house and kept crying, "What have they done to my boys?" Her cat squirmed in her wiry arms.

"I'll be back," I said to her, while the house crushed slowly into itself and was smashed and driven by the bulldozer down into its own cellar hole. I moved away and circled the crowd pressing in to see the last of the demolition through the dust. "I'll be back," I told everyone. "Don't worry. I'll come back someday. I'll come back, I promise."

The King of Spain's Daughter

LAUREL'S SANDALS WERE SIZE ten, two sizes larger than she normally wore, yet the plastic straps cut into her feet like baling wire. Swinging her legs out of the car, she pried the sandals off by levering them against each other, left them sprawled under the car, and padded barefoot into the house, her briefcase on its shoulder strap thudding against her hip.

"Oh, you little bastard," she groaned, "why are you doing this to me?" She leaned against the sink, pressing hard against the spearpoint of her breastbone with the heel of her hand to counter the pressure of the eight-month fetus, which still rode suffocatingly high in her swollen and miserable body. "Damn," she said. "I'll get you for this."

She wriggled out of her dress, peeled off the giant-size pantyhose, and stood there in harness-heavy bra and canopy slip, breathing hard, clothes pooled around her feet. She filled a glass with ice, uncorked a bottle, and poured in half a glass of red wine, then carbonated water. "Okay," she said. "Sue me." She trudged upstairs.

It was early afternoon, a warm September day. Greta, in day care, would be lying down too, taking the nap that was automatic there but a subject of fierce struggle at home. Arranging herself in a mass of pillows, Laurel could hear a woman calling some child too young for school. Most of the mothers on the block stayed home with their kids, drifting together in little herds from house to house for coffee, sharing who knows what secrets of maternal insight and feminine lore. It made Laurel feel like crying. She cried, her emotion liquid and unhinged.

She got up and went to the bathroom, then washed her face, and went once more through the long process of finding a comfortable position in bed. An elbow or knee or short pointed stick jabbed a sore spot on her intestines, and she started crying again. "This has to stop," she said. "You're too young to hate me. Listen, shhh." And she sang in a soft shallow voice:

Hushaby,
Don't you cry.
Go to sleepy, little baby

and on through to the end. She breathed hard. "Damn." She tried to remember the words of some of the songs Burney had been singing to Greta the past few days, old songs from a book his mother had sent in a box of his father's stuff, three years after his death.

"Did your folks sing these to you when you were a kid?" Laurel had asked as she unpacked the box. He took it from her and flipped through the brittle pages.

"Maybe. I don't remember the book."

Laurel read from the letter that Mary had tucked into the box. "She says it was Grandmother Nichols's. She found it in your dad's service trunk." Burney set the book aside to look through the rest of the carton – a few ribbons, a high-school yearbook, a cigar box filled with arrowheads. Laurel patted him on the back. "Are you okay?"

He shrugged. "Sure. I don't remember seeing any of this. It doesn't have any associations for me. I wish I'd known about these arrowheads when I was twelve or ten or whenever I went through my Indian phase."

Afterwards, though, he had looked more closely at the book and had even gone into the study to pick out the melodies of some unfamiliar songs on his violin. The next morning, he sang them to Greta while getting her dressed. Greta knew some of the songs already and sang along, insisting on her own words when their versions differed. She listened carefully to the songs that were new to her, then joined in, faking what she hadn't caught, the way irregular churchgoers sing the liturgy.

Although his voice was even worse than his violin playing, Burney sang all the time when he was with Greta, had done so from the time she was a baby. He was always disappointed when Greta wanted to sing some song by herself. "No!" she would say, raising her hand. "Just me." Usually they would sing together, Burney's baritone croaking and cracking beneath Greta's sweet throaty soprano.

Laurel had sung in choirs and musicals through college, but she was somehow self-conscious about it in her own home and rarely let anybody hear her. She had tried to explain it once. "It's sort of a stage thing. Here it doesn't feel right. I feel self-conscious."

"But that's crazy."

"I know it is. I'll work on it, okay? Don't harass me, Burney. It makes it worse."

The next time she needed to go to the bathroom, Laurel found the old song book and took it back to bed with her. An open window carried the sound of a baby crying, afternoon traffic noises, maple leaves drifting against the screens. She read through some familiar songs with unexpected second and third verses. One she remembered from her childhood, though as a popular song – Nat King Cole, she thought – not a nursery song:

Lavender's blue, diddle, diddle,
Lavender's green.
When I am king, diddle, diddle,
You shall be queen.

"*Dilly, dilly,*" she thought and sang softly through the next three verses. When she came to the last verse, she had to stop singing. She read to herself:

Let the birds sing, diddle, diddle,
And the lambs play.
We shall be safe, diddle, diddle,
Out of harm's way.

"I'm as bad as Burney," she said out loud, studying the mascara marks she was dabbing onto the blanket hem's frayed satin.

She paged around until she found a song she'd heard Burney teach Greta over breakfast that morning:

I had a little nut tree, nothing would it bear
But a silver nutmeg and a golden pear.
The King of Spain's daughter came to visit me
And all for the sake of my little nut tree.

She sang the song of Aiken Drum, who in this version was dressed in "good cream cheese" and "good roast beef," "penny loaves," "crusts of pies," and "haggis bags," rather than being made of pizza and spaghetti, as on one of Greta's tapes.

Somewhere in the middle of "Oranges and Lemons," Laurel fell asleep. She woke up a little later, listening to the rocking chair in the living room downstairs make its distinct *cricket-cree-cree* racket. "Burney?" she called. There was no answer, but the noise stopped. "Burney? Is that you?" Somebody was moving around. "Burney?" He almost never was home before five o'clock, and it was only three now. "Who's that? Burney?" Little rustlings.

For a minute, Laurel considered dialing 911, but in the middle of the day it seemed too stupid. Mothers were wheeling their babies in strollers right outside on the sidewalk. She went to the window. Nobody was out there at the moment.

Some small object fell over downstairs. Laurel knew the condescending looks men give to pregnant women's irrational impulses. But she also remembered the Manson gang. As quietly as she could, she pulled on a robe and went into Greta's room, where she hid herself in the darkness of a walk-in closet. And then she thought, *I was hollering up here a few minutes ago. He knows I'm here.* She left the closet, picked up Greta's portable tape recorder, and went to the top of the stairs. "I'll be down in a minute," she shouted. Counted to a hundred. Then started downstairs, with the heavy little box ready to swing, throw, smash.

"Boo!" At the bottom of the stairs, a little girl jumped out from behind the playroom door. It was Meghan, the three-year-old from across the street. "Can Greta play?"

Carefully, Laurel set the recorder on an end table in the downstairs hallway. "She's still at day care, Meghan. You shouldn't just walk into people's houses. You scared me."

"I know!" Meghan said. "Can I play with Greta's toys till she comes home?"

"No, you can't. I'll walk you home," Laurel said. "Wait here." She found some slippers, took the little girl by the hand, and walked her across the street.

Meghan's mother came around the back of her house, scolding. "Where have you been?"

"Visiting."

The woman apologized. "I hope she hasn't been bothering you. Her brothers look after her in the summer. Now that they're in school, I just can't seem to keep track of her." She gave the girl an affectionate swat on the backside and ordered her into the house. Instead, the girl headed off down the sidewalk and disappeared behind a neighbor's house. "What can you do with a kid like that?" her mother asked. "Still, you've got to love them, don't you?"

"You've got to," Laurel said.

At supper that night, Burney chewed her out for leaving the door unlocked. "It *could* have been Manson," he said. "I hope you've learned your lesson. You were lucky this time. You've just got to take better care of yourself."

He went on and on about it until Laurel laid her fork down hard and said, "Damn it, Burney. I know that. Anyway, you're to blame here too. None of this would be happening if it weren't for you. I'd be comfortable, thin. I could get through the day. My legs wouldn't ache all the time. I could *breathe*, for God's sake. This is your fault. I ache all over. I can't even breathe!"

And Greta sang out in a high clear voice: "*There was a man lived in the moon, in the moon, in the moon. There was a man lived in the moon, and his name was Aiken Drum.*"

How I Got Rid of that Stump

"AIR CONDITIONER, answering machine, clock radio, exercise bike, rowing machine, ionizer, CD player, easy chair, reading lamp, miniature reading lamp, bookcase and books, desk, computer, humidifier, television, VCR."

"Okay," I said. "I know it's a little crowded in here."

"And that's just the bedroom. In the bathroom: doctor's scale, Water Pik, Jacuzzi motor, towel warmer, soft-soap dispenser, Dixie-cup dispenser, dental-floss dispenser, bookcase, more books."

"We use all those things. They make life more comfortable. When Le Corbusier says that a house is a machine for living in, he isn't saying anything cold or unfriendly. He means it's wonderful."

"Well, she said, "I sometimes would like to live in a machine with fewer moving parts." She lay on her side, naked, head propped on her strong nurse's hand that had just done some extraordinary things to my body. She watched me hunt for a book by John McPhee I'd been telling her about at supper.

"You use machines all the time at the hospital," I said. "They save lives. They're just tools – nothing evil about them."

"Doctors use machines all the time," she said. "Nurses save lives with their hearts. Human contact."

"You saved my life a few minutes ago, Celia," I said. "Don't think I'm not grateful." An uproar of barking arose from next door, obnoxious even over the sound of the air conditioner. "God damn those beasts. I'd gun them down, I swear, if I owned a gun." I found the book, handed it to her, and lay back down and watched as she started to read. I love this time, when I've got my glasses on again and can see her, her splendid unfashionable body temporarily swept clear of modesty, acceptable to herself for even a brief time.

"I became a tuner partly because of the tools," I told her. "Instruments. Do doctors carry as many instruments in their black bags as I have in my technician's case?"

"Doctors don't have black bags anymore," she said. "Those were for house calls. I know nurse practitioners who make house calls but no doctors."

"Would they have as many instruments?"

"I can't imagine."

"Good."

"Why do *you* lug so much around with you?"

"You never know," I said. It's true that I rarely use more than a fraction of the tools in my case on a call, but I like having them with me. Besides, as I said, you never know. If I can avoid a call back, it saves me time and the customer money. Eventually, I'd like to get a van, a shop on wheels. I couldn't lift a heavier case, though if I get that Nautilus knockoff, I might build myself up to it.

When we turned the lights off, the dogs were still roaring, a pair of Dobermans owned by the troll family next door. Polished, pointed animals, they are unlike their owners in every respect except viciousness. The trolls are short, stout, pale blond people. Even their eyes are almost colorless from generations underground. All of them drive massive vehicles – Cadillacs, pickup trucks towering over traffic on oversize tires and special suspensions, four-by-fours, enormous motorcycles with fairings like ships' hulls – which they park up and down the block, so that our visitors, hiking in from wherever they've managed to find a spot, always ask who is giving the party. The trolls all live together: three grown sons, two teenaged daughters, and an older daughter who lives with her husband and two kids in a trailer they moved into the backyard last year. Also, of course, Mr. and Mrs. and a quiet old grandfather, who looks like a shriveled version of the rest of them but plays a sweet banjo on the porch and is as friendly as any man I've met.

The dogs barked and barked. They are kept on chains most of the time, since the backyard fence had to be cut, posts and all, to get the trailer in. Even trolls wouldn't let those animals run loose. Finally, after a great banging of trailer and house doors, somebody must have hauled the dogs inside, because it grew quiet, and I could once again lie peacefully in the cool darkness, listening for the faint harmonic that always begins to pulse somewhere in the air conditioner just before I fall asleep.

Early the next morning, I was working on the action of an old square Steinway that had been giving me fits for days, when I noticed one of the troll boys sitting on my boulevard elm stump, eating some doughnuts, reaching forward from time to time to pick at the rust on the bottom of his truck's door panel. He was parked facing the wrong way. The windshield was cracked, and a rag was stuffed into his gas tank in place of a cap.

I wandered out onto the front porch as if checking for the newspaper, which would not be delivered until the afternoon. "Hey, Dick," I said. He looked up at me, then drank from a quart milk carton. "The folks kick you out of the house?" He started in on another doughnut from the cardboard and cellophane carton beside him on the stump. "Say, Dick," I said, "I wonder if you'd try to avoid parking right in front of our sidewalk here. I've got to bring in pianos and stuff, and it's hard when I can't park in front of my own house."

"You've got a garage," he said. "Park in it."

"My wife parks in it. Anyway, it's easier to get to my shop from the front."

"Tough shit," he said. "It's a public street."

"Well, anyway, if you could park someplace else, I'd appreciate it."

"Sure," he said and kicked the empty milk carton toward the curb, before climbing up into his truck. He'd saved a few doughnuts for the road.

"You know," I said, "you've made yourself a Molotov cocktail there, stuffing a rag into your gas tank."

"Bullshit."

"No, it acts like a wick. One spark and you're chili mac."

"Bullshit," he said again, and the truck swung around in a clumsy U-turn, banging over the opposite curb and boulevard.

"You're blackened redfish," I called to him. "Kung pao chicken." When he was out of sight, I examined the stump. The tree had been cut down the year before, but its silvery stump was still solid and scarcely checked. I had a funny feeling about the stump. I was the one who first noticed leaves falling in July, and I had turned the tree in to the city elm watch. It's the right thing to do, but still I felt like an informer. I don't like to be a snitch, even with a tree.

Grass grew tall in the shelter of its stripped root buttresses, and sticky new sprouts kept leaping out of the base. There was a time when the city would have sent out a machine with a huge catherine wheel to grind the stump down into the ground, but now you have to pay for it yourself, and then they charge you extra to haul away the chips.

Before going back in, I stomped on the milk carton and sailed it like a crippled Frisbee into the trolls' yard. When I got back in the house, there was a message on my phone machine from the people who owned the Steinway. I'd promised to have it done the previous week, and they wanted to know how it was going. It was going badly, not so much because I didn't know what to do with it but because of what it was. The trouble with this square piano, I'd told them when I picked it up, is that it's a square piano. A dead end. They liked the way it looked, though, and insisted that I restore it.

I went back to the shop kitchen and made some coffee. Upstairs, in the half of the duplex where we live, there's a Braun roaster-grinder-drip filter machine, which seemed like an extravagance to Celia but was worth every penny. Down here in the shop, I just use an old Mr. Coffee. While the machine is going, I wander through these rooms crowded with pianos and tools – the pianos themselves in pieces, actions on benches, cases gaping open nervously or frozen with bar clamps – and feel our living space overhead, room echoing room, the dream of existence in parallel dimensions fulfilled. Hence two phone lines, two answering machines, two coffee makers, stoves, refrigerators, though I could use more space for storage in the downstairs kitchen and came close once to throwing out all the appliances left here by the former owners.

After lunch I checked the mail and found Dick's milk carton stuck between some catalogues. I approved of this, in a way. It had a neat deliberateness about it that seemed worth striving for in human relationships. The beauty of a piano's equal temperament, I once explained to Celia, lies partly in its social analogue. Since a pure tone, a perfect interval, would make it impossible to play in different keys, we deliberately deviate from purity, roughen the intervals, compromise with pattern and purpose, and finally achieve a perfect evenness of quality, a balance of imperfections more beautiful than any celestial absolute. Human relationships should be like that. It's the best we can hope for.

"I'll say," she said.

I went out and looked at the stump again. The sumo brothers were coming to pick up a seven-foot grand, and I hoped to keep the spot in front free for them. They never complain, but I ran up the block to my own car and backed it at high speed into the coveted spot. Then I returned to the stump. A farmer would use dynamite or a tractor to get rid of it. I remembered an ad in an old catalogue for a stump puller consisting of gangs of pulleys and a ratchet lever, and I would have gotten one of those, even for this one stump, if I thought they were still made, mechanical advantage is that beautiful to me.

Instead, I got my garden cart out of the garage and started moving salvaged brick from the pile beside the garage to the boulevard in front. When there seemed to be enough, I made a ring around the huge stump, then another on top of that, then another, till there was a loose wall rising well above the stump's top, six courses high.

The sumo brothers arrived in their old Chevy bread truck, so I moved my car again and let them park. Huge pinch-eyed men in monster overalls, they examined my construction, and one of them, Mike, prodded it questioningly with the toe of his boot.

"I'm going to burn that sucker," I explained. "Soak it with kerosene first. Maybe have a weenie roast." Nick, the other man, shook his head skeptically. "You don't think it'll work?" I asked. Nick shrugged. "What if I bore holes down from the sides, for draft?" Mike crouched down and ran his thumbnail along the cut surface of the stump, raising a little welt of moisture. "What if I pile a bunch of charcoal on top, let it burn down into the stump?"

"Might do," Nick said. "These bastards are son of a bitch."

When they'd loaded the piano, I went back for the legs and the lyre, phoned to make sure the owner was home, and brought some beers out to the front steps.

"So," I said to them, "what do you think about this Tatar demonstration at the Kremlin?"

"We're not Tatars," Mike said. "We're Georgians."

"Well, anyway, what do you think about it?"

"Don't think nothing about it," Nick said. "They can all go to hell, don't bother me."

"I don't understand that attitude," I said. "Don't you feel any curiosity about what's going on back there? Don't you wonder what it would be like if you had stayed and still lived there, what you would be doing?"

Mike finished his beer. "Boy, when you get your ass out of serious trouble, you just glad you can sit down anywhere. You don't concern yourself about the rest. You coming with us here?"

After splashing the stump liberally with mineral spirits, since I didn't have any kerosene, I followed them in my car and helped set the piano up in a Kenwood living room that was so big it hardly knew the piano was there. I spent an hour or so tuning and adjusting the action. When I finished, I played a piece of my own composition, which utilizes the entire keyboard. Its strangeness, perhaps, brought the woman of the house in from her garden. She sat and listened and watched while I made a few more adjustments than were really necessary.

"It sounds lovely," she said. "I'm afraid we rather let it go to pot the last few years. After my daughter went away to school, no one played it, and then the movers did something horrible to it. You've fixed all that, haven't you."

I closed my eyes and played some Chopin. It was partly a literary gesture, my becoming a piano tuner, and this was one of the moments in the story I had projected forward when considering what to do with my life, fear of blindness having blocked the artist's life I'd always planned. Eyes closed, I felt her watching, a pretty, crinkle-faced woman with a mass of frizzy hair drawn back into a huge flowing brush, shoulders sweaty, halter and shorts framing a soft friendly stomach, legs tapering sharply from broad hips to dirty feet, un-self-conscious veiny hands with earth under the nails. The huge room was cool and polished, and for all I knew we were alone in the house, with all those rooms and hours of afternoon around us. Books are full of blind piano tuners *plink-plunking, plink-plunking*, listening to bare feet shush behind them across carpets, intimate and bold, and I was full of books. Although I am relatively sighted, at times like these I still feel the touch of that secrecy, that silky robe of invisibility and permission.

"Those fellows seemed to know what to do with a piano," she said, "your movers."

"The sumo brothers," I said. "Yes, they do. I get them whenever possible."

"Sumo?"

"I can't pronounce their name. They're Russian. Georgians."

She laughed. "They do look like wrestlers. Rather terrifying."

Is that good or bad? I wondered. *What is the role of awe in sexual attraction?* They were fairly old guys, but power is power.

She walked over to the piano and the great overlapping harp of strings. She ran a hand along the hollow curve of the case. "It looks beautiful," she said. "I thought it might be a goner."

Furniture polish, I thought. I'd reattached the bass bridge, glued some loose soundboard ribs, repaired the lyre, regulated the action, voiced the hammers, and tuned. And it's the polish that gives her the most pleasure. This wasn't fair to her – she'd admired the tone – but it's the sort of thought that afflicts me in the houses of the wealthy. She went over and examined my stroboscope, which I always lug around and rarely use, except on electric pianos, and touched the handle of my tuning lever. "Now, this is lovely," she said. "What do you do with it?"

I got out some mutes and untuned and tuned a few notes for her.

"Why does it have to be so long?" she asked.

"To generate enough torque. Piano strings have around a hundred and sixty pounds of tension on them, and the pins have to hold that with sheer friction. We used to call them wrest pins, which suggests the effort of turning them. Wrest, wrestle. We used to call the tuning lever a hammer, though I can't tell you why."

"It looks a little like a hammer," she said. "I've never seen a hammer with such a beautiful handle, though."

"That's rosewood," I said.

"Yes," she said, "I see it is."

On my way home, I picked up some steaks and a giant bag of briquettes. When I got back, Celia's Volkswagen was parked in front of the house. "Why didn't you use the garage?" I asked her.

"I couldn't get the door open. Something's wrong with the opener."

"Sorry," I said. "Planes or something must have been setting it off, so I was experimenting with different codes. Forgot to reset your transmitter."

"Jesus," she said. "Airplanes open it?"

"Or something. I've been finding it open during the day. There's a lot of stuff to steal out there."

"Maybe I just forgot to close the door."

"Never."

"Cut the crap," she said. "Go fix it. I have a Greek class tonight. And what's that out front? Is bricking in the stump any solution?"

I explained my plan to her.

"Why go to all that trouble? Why don't we just pay somebody to remove it? Besides, it sounds incredibly dangerous. You soaked it with paint thinner?"

"Mineral spirits. It's just like charcoal lighter. It's not like gasoline. It won't explode. The bricks are for safety, so everything stays contained. Not that there'd be a forest fire or anything. This will work."

Eager to prove it, I ran an extension cord out to the boulevard, put a one-inch Forstner bit in my big drill, and started boring holes in the tough wood. It was heavy going, though. The bit quickly smoked and turned blue. I was afraid the mineral spirits might catch fire from the friction, but it didn't seem to have soaked in very far. The curls of wood came out hot, smelling only of their own scorching. A cheap spade bit worked somewhat better, and I managed to drill a few holes from the top, slanting through the sides, before the bit started to dull and bind. I poured more spirits into the holes, dumped briquettes in a heap that filled the space between the slope of the trunk and the straight walls of brick, soaked everything in the last of the paint thinner, and went in for a match.

Celia was upstairs in the kitchen, working on a salad. "I'm going to fire her up," I announced.

"You're going to move my car first, aren't you?"

"Of course. I came in to get your keys."

I drove the Volkswagen into the garage. After tossing half a book of matches onto the pyre, I finally got the charcoal to catch. A lot of mineral spirits must have evaporated, but as the flame crawled down, it caught more and more, until a wonderful fire roared up from the crude chimney. After a while, I balanced a grill over the bricks, charred the steaks, and had dinner with Celia. Our propane grill would have been easier, but why waste that fire?

"So," I said, "you're still thinking about going to Greece this winter?"

"I'm going," she said, "with you or without you."

"I hate to think what might happen to the house in January. Frozen pipes. Ice dams under the shingles. Trolls."

"With you or without you."

"I just don't understand why you want to leave all this comfort and convenience to go someplace where they don't even have real toilets."

"They have toilets. And if the pipes freeze, I want to be someplace else."

I sighed. "Okay, we'll go." I've always loved the idea of traveling in the Aegean. The Cyclades are magical even in their names – Naxos, Delos, Tenos, Andros. But a little reluctance now would give me leverage that might come in handy later. You never know.

"Speaking of Greece," I said, and I pushed some leftover fat and gristle into the milk carton. After dark, I would toss it into the trolls' backyard, and their Dobermans would tear it to shreds.

While she changed clothes for her class, I stood in the bedroom doorway. She's so beautiful – bony here, padded there, unexpectedly and perfectly following a pattern I've never seen in anybody else – that sometimes I can't watch her and breathe at the same time.

"You're making me nervous," she said, "staring at me like that."

"Nervous is all right," I answered. "You look Greek."

"I don't look Greek at all."

"You look like a Greek goddess."

"Demigoddess, tops," she said. "Naiad, dryad, maybe." Then she said something in Greek. "Loosely translated, that means, 'Cool your jets, dude. I don't have time right now.' "

"They teach you that sort of thing?"

"They have to," she said, "especially if you chicken out on me."

"No fear." When she was gone, I went out to make sure she'd remembered to close the garage door. Then I checked on my stump burning. The coals were covered with ash, and a fierce heat rose from the circle of bricks. It wasn't clear that the stump itself was actually burning yet, but there was a red glow visible between the briquettes, which periodically erupted into sparks and a brief flame. Smoke billowed out. I dumped some more charcoal over what was already burning and went in to work on the cracked soundboard of a Cable-Nelson upright. I try to get people to keep their humidifiers going during the winter, and I sell at cost as many case humidifiers as I can, but I still see too many of these splits. Hide glue bubbled in my electric glue pot. It's nasty, delicate work.

With the soundboard clamped, I cleaned my glue brush, swept up what would normally have been the dining room, and went from room to room, putting away tools that had been misplaced in the heat of some project, planning the next day's work. I'd finish the action of that damn square, one way or another. Start refinishing a neighbor's Chickering. Two or three tuning jobs in scattered suburbs. A good day, if I could beat the old Steinway.

It was starting to get dark when I went to check again on my stump. The trolls' grandfather sat on their front porch, playing something quick and crowded with ornament on his short-necked, four-string banjo. He showed it to me once, a beautiful old Vega that must have cost him a fortune years ago. He let me pick out a tune on it. "If you ever want to sell this baby, you let me know," I said to him.

"Won't be able to," he laughed. "I'll be dead and buried."

"Well, then, when you feel yourself slipping off, you give me a call, okay?" He'd laughed and laughed, sort of a cackle but not unpleasant.

I stood now and listened to him play. It was "Margie," one of his favorites. He stopped to wave to me, and I gestured for him to continue. "Sounds nice," I said. "How you feeling these days?"

"Strong. Real strong."

"Shoot." He laughed, increased his tempo. "All right," I said, "I believe you."

It was a quiet evening, no one out walking. Almost all the troll cars were gone, so the street looked strangely deserted. It was a hot, still evening, with distant lightning flashing and flickering soundlessly over the southern horizon. In my little fortress of brick, some equally mysterious and erratic illuminations played in and out of their own shadows. The wood must have been very wet, especially below the soil line. Wherever the coals had burned deeply into the stump, there were muffled cracks of steam pockets and an upward showering of sparks. It was quite beautiful.

When I dumped the last of the briquettes onto the burning stump, the fire seemed to withdraw, but the loose construction allowed enough draft from the sides to keep things going until the new coals could catch. I sat on the porch and listened to the intricate, insistent banjo.

After a while, I thought I heard Celia pull into the garage in back. The Dobermans, which had been quiet most of the evening, set up a stupefying racket that must have followed her from the garage to our back door. Eventually they grew quiet. I heard Celia go upstairs in back and then come down the front stairs to find me. We sat on the porch steps, sharing a drink.

"How was class?"

"Good. Some people were on vacation, so there were only three of us and the teacher."

"What did you learn?"

She said something in Greek.

"What's that mean?"

She laughed. "I'm embarrassed to tell you. I'll tell you later. When it's just us women, it gets kind of bawdy."

"Let's go inside so you can tell me."

"Later. It's nice out here. I'll tell you. Don't worry."

Dick's truck came roaring out of the darkness, double headlights blazing. He swerved over to our side of the street and parked in front of our sidewalk, facing the wrong way, and jumped out and cut across the boulevard. On the porch, he said something to the old man, who stopped his playing for a moment and resumed when his grandson went into the house.

"What did he call him?" I asked.

"Sounded like 'Ohpah.' "

"That's what I thought. *Opa*. It's what my father called his grandfather." I was ten when he died, a gray, stone-blind shadow who sat silent at the center of our family gatherings, already deep into the next world. "He pronounced it that way, too. *Opa*."

"What did you call him?"

"I never called him anything. He scared me to death."

When the banjo fell silent, we said good night to the old man and went inside. Upstairs, in bed, Celia translated what she'd said before in Greek. She was right to have waited.

Later, I remembered the milk carton. The dogs weren't around when I went out back, so I tossed the carton over the chain-link fence into a tangle of brush and weeds that had grown up behind the trailer. The dogs would find it there. They would take care of it.

Since we'd gone inside, a hot wind had sprung up, carrying the promise of storms before morning. I walked around to the front porch and saw that the added draft had gotten the coals going again. Fire was glowing through the chinks of the brick, suggesting some fantastic jack-o'-lantern's grin against Dick's insulting, backwards, rag-stuffed truck. I stood on the porch in a kind of trance and watched the sparks fly upward.

The Christmas Story

TRY AS SHE MIGHT, HIS LITTLE girl could not get comfortable sleeping with the bear that had been her heart's desire for months. The arm she draped over it arched painfully, for she could sleep only on her stomach, and the bear was bigger around than she was. "Greta, why don't you just set him next to you and sleep with your old puppy?" Burney suggested.

She snatched the dog from him and hurled it to the foot of the bed. "I hate my puppy!" she cried and tried once more to find a position that would allow her to sleep with her arms around the overstuffed bear. Finally, crying bitterly, she crawled over to the beaten old dog, tucked it familiarly under her arm, and collapsed face down into her pillow. "Cover me up," she whimpered, then fell asleep almost at once.

"Merry Christmas," Burney said to Laurel, as he waded

through the wrapping paper in drifts around the tree and settled heavily onto the sofa beside her. While she finished nursing the baby, he told her what had happened upstairs.

Laurel sighed. "Poor sweetheart. She's been asking for the bear such a long time, it must be incredibly frustrating."

"Frustration is the meaning of Christmas."

"Oh?"

"Greed, excess, disillusionment. It's a dark holiday."

"When did you arrive at that cheerful conclusion?"

He thought a moment: "1956."

"That long ago?"

"See," he said, "I worked all that year after school and Saturdays in my dad's car lot, sweeping up, cleaning windows, washing the cars – that sort of thing – to get enough money to buy a really good camera. Then my little brother wanted one too, so my folks bought him a camera for Christmas. It wasn't as good as mine, but it was a real camera. I went to bed Christmas Eve mad as hell. I'd had to *earn* mine."

"You were a jerk in those days, Burney. I'm glad I didn't know you then."

"No, usually I was generous. It's just that Christmas sets up all these expectations. I know how Greta feels."

"One avaricious moment – that sours the holiday for all time?"

"It doesn't sour the holiday. It's just a dimension."

"You said 'the meaning.' "

Burney slouched farther down on the sofa and looped one arm around Laurel's shoulders so he could stroke the sucking baby's head – downy, seamed as a baseball.

"Think about the whole story," he said. "A poor schlump of a husband who thinks maybe he's been had. An occupied country. Inconvenient travel, missed reservations, outrageous accommodations. Evil king, slaughter of the innocents – "

"Cut it out."

" 'Tis the season to be jolly."

"You're faking it," she said. "I think you love Christmas."

"There was that time in college, too," he said. "That Christmas program."

"*That* story," she said. "That *was* tragic."

"You don't know the half of it."

"The half I know is tragic."

What she knew was that in his sophomore year of college, just as he was losing the last shreds of interest in preparing for the seminary, he'd been recruited as Youth Minister of an Episcopal church in Eastchester. He'd taken the job, though, mostly out of reflex, as he had gone to a church in the South Bronx for a while to tutor disadvantaged kids and had spent a few Saturdays with mentally retarded adults from the home parish of one of his professors. These kids, at least, didn't make him feel guilty, and he could use the money.

He did little that could be considered ministry. He mainly chaperoned in the most negligent fashion the parties that evolved out of what were supposed to be Bible classes in the plush church meeting hall. He would sit on a folding chair, drink soda, and argue politics or social issues with those who were too shy or inept to dance or were momentarily between partners. Occasionally he would raise some problematic passage from the New Testament for their consideration, such as the story of the crooked steward who spreads his boss's money around just before he gets fired, then is commended by the boss for making friends with unrighteous Mammon.

One time he posed a question that his preacher grandfather had asked him when he was little: "Who is the most contemptible character in the Bible?" He had answered, "Pilate? Judas?" And his grandfather had said, "No, it was the prodigal son's older brother." Burney had been shocked at the time, and after he reminded them of the story, he was shocked by his Bible class's agreement with the judgment. "Come on," he'd argued. "*Most* contemptible? *Most*?" Another time, he told them about the doctrine of the fortunate fall, *felix culpa*, and some of the girls had started calling him that, Felix Culpa, and then just Felix, which they thought was an even funnier name than Burney. In fact, he was more dismally innocent than most of them.

Before he quit, he agreed to help the teenagers plan a folk-rock Christmas program. He wrote a script, and they pieced together a tape mixing Dylan, Buddy Holly, the Everly Brothers, Joan Baez, and Peter, Paul and Mary. He arranged to stay in his dorm an extra two nights at the end of term so he could attend. The night of the program, he had dressed painstakingly, repetitively, rummaging through both his and his roommate's closets. Then he called a cab instead of, as usual, having the pastor's wife pick him up. He waited in the falling snow outside the college gates, feeling splendid.

"Nice hat," the cabbie had said when he got in.

Burney brushed snowflakes from the fedora's softly broken crown and broad brim. "It's old," he said.

"A Stetson, am I right?"

Burney looked at the satin lining inside. "Yeah, it is."

"Best hat in the world," the cabbie said. "My old man used to have a hat like that."

Burney gazed peacefully out the window as they drove through the snowy deserted streets, past the last mansions of Bronxville into working-class Tuckahoe, past the Catholic church's life-size crèche, past bars and the bowling alley and shabby Italian restaurants, then uphill again to the prosperity of Eastchester. He reached for his wallet.

"Here you go, bud," the cabbie said. "St. Mary's Episcopal, right?"

Burney looked up. For the last few blocks he had been fumbling through his pockets – pants, jacket, overcoat, jacket, overcoat, pants. "Listen," he said, "I somehow left my billfold back in my room." The cabbie stared at him, saying nothing. Burney went through all his pockets again. "Look, give me your name, and I'll bring the fare down to the cab station tomorrow. I know where it is. I'll pay double, for the trouble," he said and laughed miserably at the rhyme.

The cabbie straightened and faced ahead where his headlights were smearing into the falling snow. He said, "You goddamn college boys. You call a cab, you got to have money. I hate being stiffed. I goddamn hate it."

Burney thought about having the cabbie drive him back to the college so he could get the money, but then he'd miss most of the program. It was probably almost eight already. Besides, after Christmas shopping the last two days, he wasn't sure he had enough money to pay for a round trip, much less a triple ride.

"You got to have money," the driver kept saying.

Then Burney thought about the hat. He said, "You like the hat, right? How about if I leave it with you for collateral?"

The driver swiveled around warily. "Collateral, huh? What size?"

Burney didn't know. While he was trying to read the worn and faded tag, the cabbie reached back, took the hat from him, and delicately slipped it onto his balding head.

"Fits perfect," he said, admiring himself in the rearview mirror.

"So it's a deal?"

"I don't give credit, bud, even with collateral. Seeing as how it's Christmas, though, I'll trade you even, ride for hat."

Burney watched the snow falling through the lights of the great church. The doors were closed, steps empty, stained-glass windows glowing. The service must have started. He knew he was being cheated, but he said, "Okay," and got out bareheaded.

The cabbie rolled down his window. "Hey, how about a tip?" Burney looked at him, and the driver laughed. "Only kidding! Merry Christmas!" he shouted and drove off, fedora tilted over his face.

While Burney was still standing at the curb, a car pulled up beside him. Elizabeth James, the pastor's wife, rolled down the window, and he crouched a little to speak to her.

"We missed you, Burney. Where were you?" She saw his confusion and said, "Oh dear, you got the time wrong, didn't you? The program was at seven. Everyone's at the reception now, in the meeting hall. Why don't you join them?"

"I don't think so," Burney said. "I feel too stupid. I think I'll just head back."

"Let me give you a ride, then. I'm going to pick up my son at La Guardia."

"I'd rather walk," Burney said. "Thanks anyway."

"Burney, the program was just beautiful. Even some of the old folks liked it. Peter is so pleased with what you've done with the kids."

"Good. I'm real glad it worked out."

"Please let me give you a ride."

"No thanks. I'd really like to walk."

"It *is* a nice night, isn't it? The snow is lovely."

"Good night, Elizabeth," he said. "Merry Christmas."

"Merry Christmas, Burney. We'll miss you."

"Merry Christmas," he said again and started the long walk back, wondering how he was going to break into his room.

That was what Laurel knew. What he hadn't told her before was that the hat hadn't been his in the first place. It was his roommate's.

She laughed, disturbing the baby for a moment. When she had got it back to business, she said, "You gave away your roommate's hat? What did he say when he found out?"

"He was really ticked off. But what could he say? It wasn't really his hat, either." That October they'd been at a funeral service on Long Island for a classmate who had been killed in a car wreck. It was a long service, with friends from high school talking about what kind of guy he'd been, and Burney and his roommate, Ron Wilke, left early so they could catch a train back into the city. While they were putting on their coats in the church cloakroom, Ron had spotted a broad-brimmed old hat on the rack, tried it on, and walked off with it.

"You let him?" Laurel asked. "That's horrible."

"I know," Burney said. "I tried to talk him out of it, but he was out of there before I knew what was happening. Afterwards, on the train, he said he'd done it for Larry, the kid who had gotten killed. That it was the sort of thing *he'd* have done. Which was probably true."

"Steal some poor man's hat at a funeral? What a bunch of goons you all were."

"Don't you see – it was sort of life-affirming." She didn't see. He got up and went to get some wine left over from supper.

He set the glasses down, took the sleeping baby from her, and lay back with the baby resting on his stomach. Larry *was* kind of a goon, he thought. On the train, they'd gotten to talking about him. Burney had remembered Larry, Ron, and a bunch of other guys from their floor coming in sick drunk from the bowling alley shortly before their first Christmas vacation. Larry had something huddled under his coat. It turned out to be the plaster baby Jesus from the crèche in front of the Catholic church. Laurel groaned.

"That was Larry," Burney said.

The little plaster figure had ended up in Burney and Ron's room, and it had looked so strange resting on a desk among term-paper notes and library books and soda cans that Burney hadn't been able to sleep. He had kept seeing the ghost-white face, the emotionless pale-blue eyes wide open, the chubby hands raised a little as if to grab something hovering in the air right above it. Finally he had gotten up, dressed, loaded the baby Jesus into his gym bag, and walked the mile or so to the church lawn, where the elaborate manger scene blazed in floodlights, with shepherds, wise men, sheep, cattle, and Mary and Joseph all focusing reverently on an empty nest of straw.

Burney unzipped the bag, made sure no cars were in sight, took the plaster figure out, and hustled up the little hill to join the crowd in the scarcely sheltering stable. As he was placing the baby Jesus into the manger, a siren started somewhere, and he jerked, knocking the baby's head against Mary's hand, breaking off her little finger. Burney dropped the baby into the manger, picked up the finger, and ran, snatching up his gym bag without stopping.

He didn't tell Laurel that part of the story. Years later, he would find the slender plaster finger in a box of old pens, buttons, shoelaces, and other trash and try to remember why he had taken it.

"Burney," Laurel said, after they'd put the baby to bed, "all those tough memories – is that why you choked up tonight when you were reading the Christmas story to us?"

He said, "Maybe." After a while he said, "No, I think it was just having the new baby there with us. After Greta was born, I couldn't watch even the most fake birth scene on television without getting blubbery." He went to check on Greta, stopping first at the nursery door. He stood there awhile, listening to the baby breathe. Then he went into Greta's room, pulled the covers up over her shoulders, and sat down on the edge of the bed. "Okay," he said to himself, "I can do this. And it came to pass in those days that there went out a decree from Caesar Augustus that all the world should be taxed. Blah, blah, blah. And Joseph also went up from Galilee, out of the city of Nazareth, into Judea, unto the city of David, which is called Bethlehem, because he was of the house and lineage of David, to be taxed with Mary, his espoused wife, being great with child."

"Okay," he thought, "no problem. Being great with child. And so it was that, while they were there, the days were accomplished that she should be delivered. And she brought forth her first-born son, and wrapped him in swaddling clothes, and laid him in a manger, because there was no room for them in the inn. And there were in the same country shepherds – okay. And there were in the same country shepherds abiding – "

And exactly as before, each time he started, emotion surged up like an enemy, choking him into silence. Love beat against his temples, fierce as migraine, and he wondered, *How did this come to be? How could he be this happy?*

The Real World

"NO MONSTERS!" THE BOY insists, his hand gripping the stock of a broken canoe paddle, which he has been using as a submachine gun. He is seven or eight years old.

"We're cavemen," a smaller boy shouts down to him from the porch, where he has made his stand.

"No monsters! No cavemen! This is the real world, with guns and tanks and grenades."

"*Arrrraghghgh!*" the second boy roars, raising his terrible arms, nine feet tall. "*Arrrrraghghghghgh!*" And the first boy, furious, aims his paddle from the hip and fills him with hot lead from the impotent real world.

The Bert and Ernie Show

It had been a freakish winter, mild and rainy, and the light snow dusting yard and sidewalk, swing set and sandbox, seemed irrelevant to Burney—a half-hearted effort coming long after anybody could take it seriously. He stood looking through the glass panel of the back door, finishing a cup of coffee, while the baby tugged at the dangling belt of his trench coat. When the belt came loose, he turned on the boy and chased him across the kitchen. The baby squealed with play terror, his knees slipping and churning, laughing like crazy when Burney caught him and struggled for the belt.

Greta pushed her cereal bowl back and chanted, "We're going to make a snowman. We're going to make a snowman. Snowman, bo bowman, fee-fie-foe mowman, snowman!"

"There isn't enough snow," he said. "Anyway, we've got to

get going. Maybe this afternoon, if it keeps up."

The girl stopped. "You said! You promised, when it snowed, we'd make a snowman. Goddamn it!"

"Watch your language," Burney said. "Didn't Hal get a time-out for saying that at school?" The jargon of preschool discipline still felt odd in Burney's mouth, but consistency, he thought, was helpful. "You want a time-out now?"

Greta started crying. Laurel, fixing the baby his breakfast, groaned. "Let's not get too involved here," she said. "I've got to finish dressing and leave in a few minutes. Can you drop Ben off at day care?"

"Maybe. I guess, if he's ready soon."

Greta wailed.

"Look," he said, "let's run outside, make some snow angels, and then grab Ben and leave. There's enough snow for angels."

"Snow angels!" Greta shouted. "All right!" She ran for her coat and boots.

"What time do you have to be at Stillwater?" Laurel asked.

"Not for another hour. My guy didn't give me a chance to get on the event letter, though, so I'll need some extra time."

"Are you going to take the appeal?"

"I don't know. Probably not. I don't know what he has in mind."

"That trial was awful for you, honey. You hate trial work. Wouldn't the appeal be just as bad?"

"I don't know. I've never done one."

"That's what I mean."

"Snow angels, bo bow angels, fee-fie-foe mow angels, snow angels!"

"In a minute, Gret."

"You know what I mean?"

Burney shook his head. "I really thought I could handle it," he said. "Somehow I kept missing something."

"It's not your thing, Burney."

"Snow angels, bo bow – "

"Okay," Burney said. "Okay." They went out into the backyard.

"How do you do this?" Greta asked. "I kind of forget."

Burney eased himself down into the light fluff of snow, stretched out, fanned his legs and arms, and carefully stood up again. "There, it's easy." His angel's outline was faint at the extremities, dark in the middle. "Your turn."

Greta shrieked, "No way! Look at your back! You're all yucky."

He twisted his loose coat around. "Shit." There was a long smear of mud where he had lain down. When they got back inside, he gingerly removed the coat and scraped at the mess with a paper towel.

"Daddy gets a time-out," Greta announced to her mother. "He got all dirty, and he said 'shit.' "

Laurel laughed. "I'll take it to the cleaners, honey. Ben's ready to go as soon as I find his cap. Greta, check for Ben's red cap when you go upstairs to brush your teeth. I think I saw it in the hallway. The car seats are in the station wagon, Burney. You want to take it?"

He disliked driving the ungainly blue Ford and would have preferred to pull into the prison parking lot in something a little less conservative, but it was a pain cramming the baby's complicated seat into the back of the old two-door Datsun and then stuffing the baby in and buckling everything. In the station wagon, it was easy.

When the three of them stepped out onto the back porch, Greta started to take off her parka. "What are you doing?" Burney asked.

"If you don't have to wear a coat, neither do I."

"I'm wearing a coat," he said. "See, this is a coat. A sports coat, they call it. I'd wear my trench coat if it wasn't muddy."

"It's not a real coat," Greta complained, but grudgingly she zipped up her parka again.

"Anyway," Burney said, "I'm just going to be in the car and then run inside. You guys will play outside today. You need a coat."

"I know that!" she shouted. "Don't keep saying it! Don't you see that my coat is zipped up?"

"Okay," he said. "Fine." He got the baby strapped in,

buckled Greta's seat belt, and cleared out the crayons and colored papers and toys that had drifted onto the floor, threatening to jam the brake or accelerator pedal. This was another thing he disliked about the station wagon – the ever-present kid mess.

Greta sang songs all the way to preschool and kissed him passionately when he was about to leave. "That yuck will wash out," she assured him. "Don't worry."

"Good," he said. "Thanks, Greta."

Burney parked near the old warden's house and pulled his jacket collar up against the wind and driving snow that had been snaking across the roads ever since he had left the city. Through the slanting whiteness, the brick walls looked softly blurred, and it took him a while to find the entrance.

With his hand stamped and three more heavy doors locked behind him, Burney entered the prison's old law library. Even this room was secured with a ponderous steel door. A young woman sitting at a table introduced herself as the interpreter, Jenny Marx. The only other person present was an inmate librarian, reading the newspaper. The room reminded Burney of his high-school library, which had, in fact, been used as a place of detention, on the assumption that troublemakers hated books. This library, though, was a place of power, its donated collections of cheaply bound advance sheets holding the secrets of the labyrinth. After a while, a guard brought in Walter Abram, Burney's armed-robbery appeal.

"They told me you've thought of a new angle for your appeal," Burney said, watching out of the corner of his eye as the woman translated his words into sign. She was graceful and relaxed, concentrating on her work, managing somehow not to be distracting, though she was effortlessly beautiful. Burney wished she had been the interpreter at the trial.

Walter Abram was Burney's age, but his thinning blond hair made him seem older. He had the sort of blue eyes that are hard to face, hard to avoid, and he looked amused and comfortable. The interpreter watched Walter closely and translated, Burney judged, a few words behind his expansive signing. "I missed you," Walter signed. "You don't have a TTY anymore. How can we shoot the breeze anymore?"

"I borrowed the portable," Burney said. "I had to give it back. What's really going on?"

"I like you, Burney. Don't you believe me?"

"Of course I believe you," Burney said. "I'm your lawyer, I have to believe you."

Walter laughed, with a sweet strange sound, and smacked Burney's shoulder. "I love this guy," he signed. She smiled and translated. Then he signed, "This idea came to me. Tell me what you think, your expert opinion. See, we say that what the judge should have allowed for is the fact that the gun was unloaded, wasn't really a gun but a sign that said, 'This is a robbery. Give me money. I'm serious.' "

Burney shook his head. "I don't get it."

"We have to stress the language problem. What could I do, go in there with an interpreter? Jenny, you go with me next time?" She interpreted evenly, unemotionally, not discriminating between comments addressed to her or to Burney.

"But it *was* a gun. We *made* the point about it not being loaded. It's still armed robbery."

Walter laughed, signed more slowly, emphatically, with more finger spelling. "No, to the hearing devils, it was a gun. For me, it was a word, a sign. Language, not weapon."

" 'Hearing devils?' "

Walter laughed and waved him past the question. "What can I do – rob only other deafies, make sure they know sign first? See, this is what we base the appeal on. They ignored the language question. I was deprived of my rights of expression."

Burney looked at the interpreter and asked her, knowing it was a breach of decorum, "Are you sure? Does this make sense?"

Walter reached across the table and grabbed him by the shoulder, redirecting his attention. "It makes sense to me." He used his fierce beautiful eyes on Burney like the threat of a knife. "It makes sense. It can cut my sentence in half. Call the whole trial into question. The interpreter was a joke."

Burney had wondered about her, a woman who struck him as rather hesitant, less easy with Walter's signing than he had expected from someone certified for court work. The interpreter he and Walter had used in preparing their case had seemed more fluent, and now, listening to Jenny, the contrast was striking. He nodded. "All right," he said. "I can't handle it, though. Appeals work is something else again. I've never done it. I'll help you find someone experienced." He looked out the heavily screened window at the driving snow. "I should have done that in the first place, Walt. I'm not really a trial lawyer. I told you that."

"No, no, I like you. You did your best. That was all I asked."

"Anyway, I'll help you find somebody really good."

"I have somebody good."

"No, I just can't do it."

"Andy Conlin."

"Andy Conlin?"

"Deaf lawyer from Washington, D.C. Very famous in the deaf community. You maybe saw him on *Sixty Minutes*. Real deafie, profoundly deaf from birth. Young man, very brilliant."

"So," Burney said, "you think he'd take your appeal?"

"Yes. He'll take it."

"Well, great. That sounds great. You want me to write him?"

"Not necessary," Walter signed. "He's going to fly out next week. You can meet him then. Very famous, very brilliant man."

"I'll do whatever I can to help," Burney said, wondering how much he'd contributed already to an appeal based on the incompetence of a hearing world to deal justly with the nation of the deaf, how much his *pro bono* eagerness had laid the groundwork of Walter Abram's real case. *All right*, Burney thought, hesitating in the entryway of the prison before slogging coatless and gloveless to his car. *Good luck to him. He's welcome to my mistakes if they'll do him any good. The law moves in mysterious ways.*

He waited for the car to warm up a little, edged out of the parking lot down the long prison drive to the road, and slued out onto the barely visible highway. It was colder than it had been before, and the snow had grown harsh, grainy, and flung itself against the windshield as if blasted out of a fire hose.

Now Burney was glad of the heavy car, which plowed through the storm in a stately and untroubled fashion. The half-hour drive would take at least an hour and a half, given the rate of the sparse traffic. Burney listened to the radio, tightened a window against the splinter of cold air that carried little bullets of snowflake against his cheek, sang, signed through the alphabet. He'd picked up a little American Sign Language and gestured now "be cool," "see you later," "any questions?" "good luck." "Good luck!" he signed, and while his hand was off the wheel, the car skidded a little, fishtailed left and then right, caught the edge of a drift, and slid nose-first down a long embankment, gaining speed.

When Burney came to, it had begun to get dark. Snowflakes still whirled around the top of the cracked windshield, visible in the few inches of glass not yet drifted over. Burney's forehead had bled a little and now was clotted and sticky. When he turned the ignition, the starter just whined and then stopped altogether. He sat there in the darkness, vaguely dizzy, examining by faint dome light the toys and papers spilled over the dashboard.

Burney knew enough to stay with the car. It was getting cold inside, though. In the back, he found an old receiving blanket, which he wrapped around his neck and tucked into the front of his jacket. Then he shoved the door open to check the damage. The car was utterly stuck, he observed, standing with his hands thrust deep into his jacket pockets. There were no lights from the highway visible through the storm, but he thought if he could scramble up the embankment, he might be able to flag down a snowplow or something. After an almost snowless winter, they would be out in force.

He crawled back into the car and looked for stray gloves or mittens under the seats, but the closest he could come, among the toys and trash, was a pair of hand puppets, which Greta had been given for Christmas. He would need to use his hands to get up the hill, so he pulled on the two puppets and wiggled his fingers into the flannel arms and the plastic heads. "Okay, Bert?" he said. "Okay, Ernie." The round-headed Ernie puppet fit his hand better than the narrow cone-shaped Bert, but both had long gauntlets that would keep the snow out of his wrists. "Let's go!"

Burney's leg bothered him a little, while he worked his way up the steep embankment, squinting into the blizzard, but it wasn't broken or even sprained. It worked. It kept moving, and he moved slowly upward, slipping, floundering in drifts, making pretty good progress where the wind had swept the weed bristle clean. At least it felt as if he were making good progress, but the embankment rose and rose, the highway always eluding him, higher in the darkness and slanting snow, the earth not yet leveling off. Gravity guided him, pulling him back. "Jesus, Bert," he grunted, pausing, "something's wrong here."

"You can say that again, Ernie. Hih-hih-hih."

And then the embankment crested. Burney staggered forward toward the road and slammed headlong into a wall that rose suddenly out of the night and storm. He stood again and felt cautiously ahead with his puppeted hands. He found the wall, glass, stretching out on either side quickly out of sight. It was a greenhouse. He'd climbed in the wrong direction, away from the highway. But this was better than he'd thought. He knew where he was. He'd find shelter here.

After creeping and patting his way completely around the greenhouse, he was unable to see any other building or light, and he was afraid to leave the greenhouse, fearing he'd get lost in a forest of arborvitae and blue spruce or in the simple open fields he remembered stretching out from the nursery.

He worked his way back to the entrance and again tried the door that he knew to be locked. He was shivering wildly. He had to get inside, but it isn't easy to break a pane of glass with your hand, even protected by the plastic head of a puppet. The spirit holds back, softens the blow. Finally, using more violence than would have seemed necessary, he smashed a pane, reached in, and got the door open.

No smother of warm moist air met him as he stepped inside, no ranks of mysterious plants breathing in the darkness, only cold black stillness. He found a rag of burlap to stuff into the broken pane to stanch the blast of storm. He moved cautiously up and down the paths between the empty benches. "At least we're out of the wind," he said.

He found a bale of straw in the darkness, kicked it apart until he could pull the straw loose from the twine, and made a nest for himself to curl up in. The effort warmed him, and he was relatively comfortable for a while and even dozed, until he started to shiver again. He looked at the faint glow of his watch. It was only seven o'clock. The colon separating hours and minutes flashed steady as a pulse. He thought with longing of the car and the drifts of crayoned paper, which he could have used to start a fire. Straw would burn, and the benches were wood. He could turn the frozen darkness of the greenhouse into a huge lantern, visible for miles, tropical and brilliant. If he had matches. If he smoked. He made another circuit of the building, gathering leaf litter and moss and rotten burlap, scooping it all up between awkwardly puppeted hands. When he tried barehanded, his fingers quickly stiffened and grew numb. His toes already had no feeling. He scoured the darkness, adding to his nest, until his head throbbed and he started to feel nauseated, exhausted from the work and the cold.

Nestled into the mound of debris, his knees drawn up under his chin, Burney smacked blood into his hands and sang some songs to keep himself awake. He clapped his hands again and furiously worked his fingers inside Greta's puppets. "Well, Bert," he said, "we're in a fix now."

"You can say that again, Ernie."

Greta hadn't liked the puppets much when she first got them, her desire had been so focused on a stuffed bear she'd been promised. But when Ben reached the point of being susceptible to entertainment, his explosions of watery laughter themselves became objects of desire, and Greta found that the puppets set him off like magic. Locked in his car seat, he was a boundlessly appreciative audience for the shows she performed for him, with Bert and Ernie improvising long dialogues on the subjects of the day. She kept them always in character – Bert the straight man, a little slow, not getting the most outrageous pun at first, laughing tightly when he did, Ernie more confident and clever.

"Bert, bo dert, fee-fie-foe mert, Bert?"

"What, Ernie?"

"Why did the warden stop sending his shirts to the prison laundry?"

"I don't know. Why?"

"Because he could never figure out what to do with the extra button."

"Extra button? I don't get it, Ernie."

"Me neither, Bert. A guy told me that one today."

The storm crashed against the greenhouse, rattling the panes so violently that it was almost impossible to conceive that the spidery shelter could survive. Before leaving the prison, Burney had tried to call home, but either the lines were down or the circuits were overloaded. Laurel probably would assume he had stayed, waiting out the storm, drinking coffee and joking with the guards in the employees' cafeteria. She always overestimated his good sense. Even if she got through to the prison, it was likely that, without an event letter listing him, nobody would be able to tell her when he'd been there or when he'd left.

"Extra button?" Bert said. "Extra button?"

Suffering as much from tedium and loneliness as from the awful cold, Burney painfully stood up, shedding his carefully arranged nest, and climbed blindly onto one of the benches. Edging forward, his hands raised high, he finally felt Bert's tall head graze against something yielding. Jumping as high as he dared, he caught a fold of the gauzy fabric that had been hung to protect plants against sunscald, and he gradually pulled it free. He felt his way back to the mound of debris and worked his way under it again, using the fabric to keep a little space clear in front of his face. He kept his hands close to his chest and wriggled down into the nest, allowing straw and trash to cover as much of the cloth as possible. When he stopped moving, he felt himself go lightheaded. His legs became leaden. Activity warmed him, but he hadn't enough energy to sustain it now. He'd have to stay put.

Imprisoned by glass and mulch, cold and exhaustion, Burney wondered how convicts endured separation from their families. He kept moving his fingers. "I want visitors," Bert moaned, absence aching like pulled teeth. "I want to hold my kids again. I want Laurel."

Checking his watch, Burney plotted like a mariner their various positions. Now the children would be getting their baths. Now they would be in the kitchen, Greta having a bedtime snack. Now, back upstairs, Laurel would be putting them to bed, and now Greta would be searching her out, wanting to be held while Laurel dialed and dialed, getting no answers. Laurel would be holding Greta now. And now. And now the baby.

Burney woke a little crazy, stupid with cold, the blood moving through his brain too slowly for the flicker and flash of thought. If he had not buried himself so well, he would have crashed out of the greenhouse and staggered toward home. He wanted to, willed it, but Bert held his right hand, and Ernie held the left, until the impulse grew quiet.

"*What* family?" Ernie whispered then. "Are you joking? Wife? Kids? *You*?"

And Bert put his arms around him and said, "It's a mystery, Ernie. I never meant to hurt you."

Invisible in the darkness, they wrestled. If a whirlwind had uncovered them, it would have revealed them in an embrace, locked like wrestlers or lovers, cone head and round head, and one carried hidden the stamp of freedom, and one did not.

It had stopped snowing, and the wind that scoured over the greenhouse roof revealed stars here and there and a half-moon, blurred by whitewash. Without clouds to capture the small warmth left in the earth, it would grow truly cold now, heat leaping out toward the stars in unhesitating abandon. Snow was drifted against the walls too high to see anything but sky outside, but the thin light made the greenhouse itself visible, an icy uninviting web of crystal and lead, its benches stretched out like a banquet of emptiness.

They slept through the night the intent sleep of buried ones. In the morning, the state patrol would probably have found them, if the nurseryman's collie had not leaped away at first light from the valley where the farmhouse was sheltered and dove and tumbled through the crusted drifts up to the glass houses on the hill, if the dog had not been tracked by the nurseryman's daughter, clumsy on snowshoes she had been given for Christmas and never used till now, if the dog had not yanked the burlap rag out of the broken pane and had not howled ecstatically at the strange still mound inside, if the girl had not let the dog in, to spring in a fury of long blunt claws.

The dog found Ernie first, snatched him out of the mound's thrilling smells, and shook the puppet's cloth body like a rat. When the girl shouted and wrestled Ernie away from him, he barked thunderously and dug again and this time found a man shrouded in white and went really wild, twisting and whirling until his long fur blurred.

The girl hauled the dog aside, brushed peat moss and bark from the man's face, and touched his cheeks, first with her mittens, then with her bare hands. His skin felt cold, stiff. Bert, hidden till now, jerked in his sleep. The girl stepped back. And then everything was pain and light and a shattering racket that thundered over Burney like an avalanche of roaring life.

I Was Picked Up by Jeanette Rankin

THE TELEVISION QUIZ-SHOW host says to the contestant who has chosen U.S. history for five hundred dollars, "She was the first woman to be elected to the United States Congress. As a member of Congress, she voted against U.S. entrance into both world wars."

Watching at home, I answer, "Jeannette Rankin."

None of the contestants pushes a buzzer, and the host reads the correct response: "Who was Jeannette Rankin?"

I say, "I was picked up by Jeannette Rankin."

In the early summer of 1971, I woke before sunrise in a field of chest-high weeds outside Amarillo, between the steep slope of the highway embankment and what must have been an oil refinery, a distant mountain of pipes and tanks that had been lighted like a city the night before, when I'd picked my way into the field to find a spot to sleep.

After jamming my dew-soaked sleeping bag into its pouch, I slipped into the pack straps and climbed, stiff from cold and the knotty ground, back up to the shoulder of the highway, heading west.

My sister was working in the Farm Workers' Union clinic in Delano, California. I was a graduate student on my way from Indiana to visit her. It was Sunday, and I expected a long wait in the dawn fog. There was little traffic – mostly families packed solid for vacations and solitary old ladies on their way to church. But while I was still settling my pack beside me and unfolding my CALIFORNIA sign, a car slowed, stopped about a hundred feet ahead of me, and backed recklessly, gears whining, to where I was hurriedly repacking my sign and gathering up my pack. A young man of about my age, wearing a blanket on his shoulders, came around from the driver's side. "You look all right," he said to me.

"I am all right," I said. I looked into the car. An old woman, tiny, also wrapped in a blanket, turned slightly, stiffly around from the passenger side and looked at me and smiled crookedly from behind harlequin glasses. The car, in my memory, was something like a 1950 Dodge. I loaded my pack into the trunk, which already contained a suitcase, a sleeping bag, and a red Gerry backpack like my own.

"I noticed your pack," the young man said. "That's why I stopped. Can you drive?"

Sure, I could drive, I answered.

"You drive then," he said. "I'm sleepy. We've been going for hours already."

I slid into the front seat and began fumbling for the pedals and the ignition. The young man climbed into the back, which was piled with cardboard boxes. Before clearing a space for himself to stretch out, he leaned forward and introduced himself as John and the old woman as Jeannette. She looked at me somewhat cockeyed from behind her large thick glasses. "While I sleep, you'll have to tell him about your time in Congress," John said, and she smiled crookedly and said something so slurred that I could not understand it. Besides, I was still trying to figure out the gearshift.

John arranged himself on the back seat, and I turned the car cautiously onto the empty highway. The old woman sat quietly beside me. After a few miles, her eyes started to close. She laid a thin, frail hand on my arm and told me – I barely understood, though I was listening more carefully – that she was going to make use of my shoulder, and she fell asleep with her gray, scarf-wrapped head resting lightly against me. I felt honored, as I did a few hours later in Tucumcari when the old woman took my arm to cross the highway from a filling station to a restaurant for breakfast.

I did not know who she was. I had not heard of her, had not understood John's vague references to her past or her own blurred comments. At the moment, I was concerned less with history than with getting to California as quickly and cheaply as possible and did not much wonder about whatever quiet craziness might be shared by these two friendly, blanketed characters, momentary supporting players in my own absorbing drama. On the road, the people who tell you their life stories, who pick you up for that purpose, are usually salesmen who have been in thirty-eight states and the District of Columbia, who are having trouble with their wives or haven't had an argument in eighteen years of marriage, who have the greatest kids in the world or are worried about a son or daughter who just can't settle down. You don't really pay attention, or, rather, the attention you pay in exchange for the ride is cheap, jerrybuilt, already falling apart while you are crouched over saying thanks, good luck, and thinking about the next ride.

The old woman was Jeannette Rankin, the first woman elected to the United States Congress, a Montana suffragette elected to the House of Representatives in 1916 and again in 1940. She had been one of the fifty representatives who voted against entering the First World War, and she had voted, alone in all of Congress, against entering the Second World War, thereby earning contempt, vilification, and then an almost magic invisibility that washed over her life.

She did not tell me her life story. Almost everything I know about Jeannette Rankin I learned afterward. Maybe she would have said more if her speech had been less difficult. John told me that she was recovering from a stroke suffered earlier that year. I didn't know enough to ask questions, and I only gradually pieced together enough remarks, mostly John's, to understand what she did say. She said once, speaking laboriously, drooling slightly from her stroke-slack mouth, "I was elected in time to vote against World War One, and they reelected me just in time to vote against World War Two. Watch out if I'm elected again." She said nothing about the twenty years between the wars, the twenty-five after – the years between filled with speeches and marches, the years after cloaked in obscurity following that incredible, second, lonely nay. Her third long day began in the sixties, with the country catching up to feminism and caught up in still another war. When I met her, she was ninety-one years old. She would die two years later.

She gave me a slogan button, the cheap kind with a folding metal tab. The print was partly rubbed off already when she fished it from her purse. It said, GOVERNMENTS MAKE WAR. She was not an anarchist. The button represented only one premise in a syllogism. The second premise was "Governments are run by men." Feminism and pacifism were one thing for her. Although some argumentative part of me squirmed, I hooked the button on my shirt pocket and thanked her.

That is practically the full extent of what Jeannette Rankin told me as we crossed the endless dry hills and flatness of New Mexico in the old car loaded with boxes of printed materials, mimeographed fliers, position statements. John had met her in Georgia while working on an antiwar protest and had become her secretary and traveling companion. They were driving to Los Angeles, where various political groups had invited her to speak. John said that I could travel with them as far as Barstow if I cared to stop when they stopped. After Barstow, they would take Highway 15 south, and I could continue west to Bakersfield and then north to Delano. I felt lucky: it would be a good long ride. I would make good time.

Every hour or so as I drove, John, awake now in the front seat with Jeannette Rankin dozing between us, would take out a portable tape recorder and talk into the microphone – a practice that interested and embarrassed me. He spoke mostly of our itinerary, describing the landscape, which was mostly unexceptional, as were his observations. When we entered a region of high stone ridges, too steep for hills and too small for mountains, I remarked that they were shaped like waves, frozen into stone. "That's pretty good," he said. "Frozen waves." He flipped on his recorder and reported that we were passing what looked like brown frozen waves.

After Tucumcari, John drove. We reached Albuquerque around noon but didn't stop for lunch. They seemed to live on dried dates and fresh fruit, which they carried in camping boxes and plastic bags and which they shared with me. From John I learned how to handle sticky dates in a hot car when there is no water for washing: you dust them with powdered milk until they separate from one another. It worked fine, and I was grateful to have learned something.

We passed the continental divide and Gallup in the early afternoon, and even before reaching Arizona we began seeing signs of the Petrified Forest – trading posts, souvenir shops selling old stone wood, dinosaur replicas. Because neither John nor I had ever been to the Forest, he decided we should stop there. If the Grand Canyon had been closer, we would have gone there too, and John regretted that we could not.

Jeannette Rankin did not say much as we took the Petrified Forest National Monument exit, but she made it clear that she had very little use for sightseeing, that there was something almost criminally frivolous about national parks, and that people who visited them while the nation itself was in such serious trouble were frivolous people. When we pulled into one of the parking areas, she would not get out, refused even to move into the shade of the information center, staying stiffly on the front seat of the car, baking under the desert sun.

I must have felt guilty, and John might have, but we gathered brochures at the information center as if we were responsible only for ourselves. I stayed in the building after John had gone outside. There was a huge mural depicting the geological history of the Petrified Forest: the fernlike, palmlike trees growing, dying, being washed into immemorial rivers, buried under miles of accumulating silt, cell by cell replaced by mimicking minerals, then the upheavals of the earth, seabeds thrust up into mountain ranges, mountain ranges worn down to plains, and the transubstantiated trunks exposed once more to the sun. The scale of space and time was smothering, dizzying, and I followed John outside to the markered paths with a feeling of oppression that only gradually left me.

I caught up with him, and we stayed together, clambering among the hills and gullies in which were lodged the random fallen pillars of stone logs. Along the paths, there were signs explaining the age and nature of the mineral formations jutting out of the desert. Other signs warned against disturbing or removing the rocks, a federal offense. In the face of the temptation to pocket a souvenir, I kept my hands out of my pockets and watched the park rangers, who were never watching me. John had brought his camera, and on a stone bridge formed by a great log lying across an arroyo he took a picture of me, and I took one of him. "I'll send you a copy," he said, but I never received it, having neglected to give him an address.

After an hour or so, we had had enough. We climbed back to the road and found the car, with Jeannette Rankin sitting exactly as we had left her, waiting out the frivolity of recreation and youth.

When you leave the Petrified Forest, you pass a small building that looks like a tollbooth. A ranger asks you if you have disturbed or removed any rocks, and you tell him you have not, and he allows you to leave. I was in the back seat, paying little attention, as John pulled up at the window of the booth, and the bored, beefy park ranger asked if we had disturbed or removed any rocks from the area.

And politely and promptly John replied, "I cannot tell a lie," and he laid on the windowsill of the ranger booth a little brown pebble, about the size of a navy bean, indistinguishable from pebbles you might find almost anywhere in the world. "Here it is," John said. The ranger looked down at the pebble for a few moments and then looked at John. Was John aware that it was a federal offense to disturb or remove materials in the national monument area? John was aware. "Look," John said, "notice that I returned it. It's just a little joke. I'll bet nobody else has ever answered yes to that question in the history of the park."

The ranger looked at him, looked down at the pebble, and said, "Pull over to the side. I'll have to search your car."

We pulled over and waited, sweltering, while the ranger asked the people in two more cars whether they had disturbed or removed materials in the park. Apparently they had not: he waved them through. Then he stepped out of the booth and walked over and told us to get out. John and I obeyed, but Jeannette Rankin stayed where she was, ignoring him. "You'll have to get out, ma'am," he said, standing stolidly beside the open door. A few more cars stopped at the gate, and he walked slowly back to give them that easiest of quizzes, which we had failed.

While the ranger was gone, John tried futilely to convince Jeannette Rankin to cooperate. When the ranger returned and insisted again that she get out before he searched the car, she growled in her stroke-slurred voice, distinctly enough, "I am sitting on a rock. I will not get out and let you discover it." Finally she did get out, slowly, painfully, with a deep, still fury in her body. She stood a ways off as the ranger stuck his head into the car, made a show of shoving a few things around, and looked perfunctorily in the trunk. "I may have a stone in my shoe," she warned him. Wasn't he going to search her shoe? She asked him who his congressman was. He said he didn't know, but Barry Goldwater was his senator. He let us go.

There was a great silence in the car as we returned to the highway and headed west again. John apologized to us. I assured him the ranger had no sense of humor. Jeannette Rankin said nothing.

It was getting dark when we reached Flagstaff, climbing through hills of small evergreens and cooler air that refreshed us after hours of bare, blasted rock and sand. There was a motel on an outlook above the highway. "It's beautiful here," John said. "Let's stop here for the night." I hoped there would be a place in the surrounding woods where I could camp. I couldn't afford motels.

We drove up the winding roadway to the motel and parked, but for the third time that day Jeannette Rankin refused to get out of the car. "I will not spend the night in a motel in Arizona," she said. "Not after the way we were treated this afternoon. You may go in. I will stay in the car. I will not contribute to the economy of Arizona. I will stay in the car."

I went into the motel to make a long-distance phone call to my sister. John seemed uncomfortable arguing with Jeannette Rankin in my presence. She had not said one word of reproof to him and yet was punishing him for indulging his impulses first to sightsee and then to play a joke, impulses blameworthy not because they had caused her discomfort but because they delayed the serious business she had been about for sixty years. I fooled around by the motel entrance while they sat and talked. They were at it a long time. Finally John drove up and told me to get in. *This time she's won*, I thought, shaking the dust of Arizona from my shoes.

It was almost midnight when we reached Kingman, still an hour's drive from the California line. And now Jeannette Rankin gave in, so tired she must have been in pain for hours. It was a clear, cool, moonlit night. John checked Jeannette into a single room, while I waited beside the car in the circular drive of the motel courtyard and watched a little fountain in a turquoise wading pool. We ate at an all-night diner. Then John and I got our packs from the car and hiked out into the desert across the highway from the motel. Beyond the lights of the cars, we unrolled our sleeping bags in a shallow depression mined with cactus and talked before falling asleep. We each told the other a version of what we wanted to be.

I think that night John felt the burden of the honor of

being Jeannette Rankin's companion. It seemed to have been a while since he had talked with someone his own age. Besides age, we had little in common, beyond a certain fondness for the outdoors, his stronger than mine. And yet that night we felt like brothers.

In the morning, we could see the great bowl of mountains around Kingman. We loaded our packs into the trunk, and I walked down the highway to a filling station to wash up, while John woke Jeannette Rankin. I waited a long time there, and it crossed my mind that they were truly crazy and that I had seen the last of them, along with my new pack and sleeping bag. But they came. We crossed the Colorado River into California around eight o'clock, had breakfast in Needles, and reached Barstow by noon. We shared a leisurely, rather regretful last meal there, on the outskirts. Then they dropped me off at what turned out to be the wrong side of town.

I hiked across town in a heat I had never experienced before, stopping at a filling station every block to drink my belly full of water, which seemed to evaporate at once. A salesman in an air-conditioned Oldsmobile took me across the desert, past Boron, Mojave, and Monolith, to Bakersfield. From there, a young woman, a grower's wife, a student nurse who wanted more than anything else to get a ten-speed bike, drove me to Delano and took me right out to the Farm Workers' Union clinic, though it was out of her way. There I saw gray squirrels racing from hole to hole in a treeless plain of dust, their bushy tails surrounded by aureoles of light in the unbelievable sun.